Beyond the Mist

By Heather D. Veinotte

ISBN-978-0-9734559-6-0

In memory of my dad,
Donald R. Ramey

Dedicated to my husband,
Bruce M. Veinotte
Who will always be the wind beneath my wings.

"HOLY MOTHER OF God, this is a bad one!", shouted the innkeeper trying to be heard above the cracking of the lightening.

"Thank God the stagecoach got here when it did."

His hands trembled, as he hung sodden wool garments on iron hooks by the door. Crouching by the window, he gaped through the small panes of lead glass as angry waves battered the rocks too close to the road and inn for safety.

He spoke to no one in particular, but the four men and three women who sat huddled on the worn benches close to the smoking fire, nodded in agreement.

Thunderbolts of lightening zigzagged across the sky illuminating even the darkest corner of the low-beamed room. Pewter tankards vibrated together on the wide oak shelves behind the bar.

Outside, torrents of rain rattled on the roof sounding as though thousands of pebbles from Maders Cove were being hurled from an enraged sky. It was as if the storm gods had decided to battle to the death above the village of Mahone Bay.

Someone was pounding on the door. The wide spruce planks almost buckled from the force of the pummeling, sounding as though the devil himself was knocking to get in.

Without warning, the door flew open and smashed against the wall. A woman screamed. Another wept in fear. There in the opening stood an outline of a man. His huge frame filled the doorway.

The innkeeper sprang into action. He grabbed the door, pushing it shut with his body.

"Come in man! Get out of the storm."

The stranger nodded, stomping to the blackened granite rocks of the fireplace. Thick, black hair covered most of the weathered flesh on his face and head. His patched coat, tattered and ripped at the hem, dragged along the floor. He removed the soaked garment revealing a large canvas bag strapped to his back. Rivulets of water coursed from the saturated overcoat to the floor and ran into the hearth causing the fire to hiss and spit. Easing his body down into the hollow of the bench, he shrugged the bag from his back and pushed it between his worn hobnailed boots.

The innkeeper pulled a tankard of ale from behind the bar.

"It's been a while since you've darkened my doorway. I thought you'd gone from these parts."

He walked to the fire and picked up empty tankards. He spoke to the passengers of the stage coach.

"It's not up to me to be telling you what to do, but the way this storm is raging, it would be better to stay in front of this warm fire than go to bed. If the lightening hits us, you won't stand a chance upstairs. I'm stayin' down here and you're welcome to do the same."

He threw another pine log into the flames. The men nodded, while the women retreated further into the back of the benches, watching the stranger warily.

The innkeeper removed a wooden lantern hanging from the beam above the bar with one hand and held the tankard of ale in the other. He walked back to the smoking fire, placing the ale and lantern on a small table by the stranger's right hand.

"A drink for a story my friend. It's gonna be a long night."

The stranger nodded, leaned over and pulled his canvas bag out from under the bench. He loosened the drawstring and pulled out a tattered leather-bound book filled with handwritten pages. Enormous calloused hands gently smoothed the cover. He grasped the handle of the tankard and took a long deep swallow, wiping his mouth with

3

the back of his hand. Piercing eyes stared at the passengers from beneath grizzled brows. Almost reverently, he opened the book to one of the ragged pages.

The stranger began to read. His rich baritone voice captivated them. The innkeeper smiled. He watched their faces relax. This had happened so many times before. Fears and prejudices for this strange giant of a man were soon forgotten as they were enchanted by this pied-piper of words. His hypnotic voice carried them away from Zwickers Inn and the raging storm, into the realms of apparitions and the supernatural...

Shipwrecked

"LOOK OUT, the mast is goin'!", the first mate screamed above the howling wind and pounding rain.

The "Catherine Rose" faced her cold Atlantic foe with only one of her three masts still standing. Cold, briny water surged through the gaping holes in her hull causing her to roll from side to side in the treacherous tidal waves. Timbers moaned and groaned with each relentless pounding of the elements.

"Captain! She's headin' for the rocks. I can't hold her!"

He hung on to the wheel with all the strength he had left in his body, but it was useless. Demonic waves surged over the side of the deck. Wet, massive arms grabbed the first mate from the ship's wheel and dragged him screaming to a watery grave.

Horror stricken, the old man watched as the sea claimed his crew one by one. The ship rolled again almost throwing the captain overboard. Heaving his body up between the broken railings of the vessel, he crawled on all fours toward the ship's wheel; the wind and rain battering his body every inch of the way. Exhausted, he lay for a moment listening to the heartbeat of the ship. Using every last bit of strength, he pulled himself to an upright position and lashed his body to the wheel. His breath coming in short fierce gasps.

In the middle of this fury and destruction, agonizing pain tightened around the brave old man's heart and he whispered his last words to the only woman he had ever loved.

"Farewell my Catherine Rose, farew..."

On the lower deck, Emma Hardwick screamed as the wounded vessel rolled on its side and cold salt water sloshed over her. The careening of the ship threw the terrified woman from a lower bunk. Her head snapped against the uneven boards of the floor as agonizing pain engulfed her.

Enveloped in complete darkness, she crawled back to the bed and felt blindly for her wool cape. Numb fingers located the heavy clasp and she pulled with all her might.

The cape and the floor moved at the same time, throwing the petrified woman against the opposite wall of the cabin. Pain seared into her arm and shoulder as the heavy iron hinges of the cabin door dug deep into her body. Still clutching the soaking cape, Emma wrapped it around her shoulders.

She pulled herself up, hanging on to the latch of the door; only to be thrown to the floor again as the ship endured another roll. More water poured in transforming the small room into a watery tomb.

"Help me! Please help me! I'm down here!"

She cried out, but in her heart she knew that no one could hear her above the howling of the wind. Outside the roar of the waves and the pounding rain battled for supremacy.

Emma, fighting against the rising waters and the heaving ship, desperately searched for the elusive door. Inch by inch she felt along the walls until numb frozen fingers fumbled against the obscure latch.

"Come help me! Please come help me!"

Screaming and sobbing, she slammed against the solid oak door. Her spent body a human battering ram.

Her muscles screamed in pain as the door finally gave way. With every fiber of her being, Emma shoved one last time and was hurled into the black, wet passage that led to the deck of the ship.

Sprawled on her stomach, with her face partly submerged in foul tasting water, she gasped for air.

Her eyes strained to pick out the smallest outline, but she saw nothing.

She sobbed in complete despair.

"Oh my God, I'm going to die!"

Digging into the very depths of her soul for strength, she crawled on her stomach searching. Emma groped until her hand struck the bottom rung of the ladder and pulling herself up, she began the agonizing climb. Crawling over the last rung, she collapsed face down on the deserted deck.

Outside the waves lashed against the bow of the ship pushing it closer and closer to the jagged rocks that beckoned like black, rotting teeth of some ancient mythical sea monster.

Finally, the "Catherine Rose" could fight her savage enemies no longer. With a final heave, the gallant ship rolled one last time. She surrendered to the waiting rocks, joining the others that had gone before her to their briny grave off the coast of Lunenburg.

There was no one left to hear Emma Hardwick's terrified screams.

Small bobbing lights rolled and swayed above the dunes like a chain of fireflies in the early light of a watery dawn. The lighthouse keeper at Battery

Point sent a message that a ship had been wrecked and help was needed. Soon after, the men of Blue Rocks came carrying their lanterns following a two-wheeled ox cart and a horse drawn wagon.

The sight that greeted the small band of men as they reached the crest of the dunes, compelled Reverend Cochrane to drop to his knees and cross himself. The rest looked on in horror at what the storm had left in its wake.

Scattered on the dark gray sand, were the lifeless bodies of the crew thrown up to the high watermark. They were flung around like grotesque rag dolls made from suttles. Broken timbers and debris littered the shore. In the sheltered cove, with soft waves lapping against a gapping hull, were the skeletal remains of a three-mast schooner.

James Tanner stopped short. The two oxen nudged him in the back. He turned around to his brother, Robert, who had followed him with the horse and wagon.

"Holy mother of God, Robbie did you ever see so much sorrow in all your life?"

Robbie shook his head, hardly able to take in the view from the top of the dunes.

"Not for a long time and I hope I never have to see it again. Let's get this hellish chore over with so we can get back to the village."

Both brothers squared their shoulders and called to the other men who were waiting in the background for the Tanners to give them their lead.

It was a gruesome task, for the rocks had not been kind to the bodies. With each corpse they collected, the small spark of hope they clung to for finding survivors flickered slowing away.

By midmorning the task was almost finished. The horse and wagon had left for the village and with it some of the men. The last body collected was the old man, still tied to the ship's wheel. The toll of life was fourteen in all.

Not much was known about the ship that lay in the cove. They knew her name for they found a board half buried in the sand with "Catherine Rose" painted in bold green letters. Broken chests of tea and planks of exotic woods lay smashed in the rocks and among the ship's timbers. They supposed she was a cargo ship bound for England from the West Indies, but without the Captain's log her owner and destination would remain a mystery.

The sun was already high in the cloudless sky. Turquoise water lapped against the rocks from the incoming tide. Most of the men had returned to Blue Rocks following the horse and oxen with their heartbreaking loads. Robbie stared at the calm waters and shook his head in awe.

"How could something so peaceful become a banshee from hell in a matter of moments?"

Jamie watched his brother stop, place his hands on his hips and search the rocks.

"What's botherin' you Robbie?"

Robbie tried to keep his balance while standing ankle-deep in drying sand.

"I thought I saw somethin' out by the rocks, but I guess I was mistaken."

He strained his eyes.

"No! There it is again. Do you see it Jamie?"

He pointed toward the rocks.

"Over by the seaweed."

He started running down the beach.

Jamie stood with his hands shielding his eyes.

"Be careful Robbie. The tide is comin' in and you know how deep those pools are by the rocks."

Robbie ran the length of the beach, never taking his eyes off the spot where he first saw sparks glinting in the sun. His heart beat faster as he approached the deep tidal pools. Reddish brown seaweed swirled and swayed with the incoming tide, beckoning him closer and closer, wanting to share its treasure with him. Soon, he was close enough that he could see what was shining in the sun.

It was the large clasp on a woman's cloak. Robert moved closer. To his horror, he discovered a body wrapped in the wet wool.

"Jamie, get down here! I found another body."

He tried to pull it from the sucking seaweed, but her tangled cape was making the rescue almost impossible.

By the time Jamie waded out to the rocks to help his brother, the water was creeping up to their chests.

"The tide's comin' in fast. You've got to let her go."

Robbie shook his head.

"I won't. The sea's not going to claim her again. Help me Jamie, pull one last time with me."

Both men tore at the kelp until the seaweed relinquished its treasure; the cape still tangled among the rocks.

They were able to drag the body out of the water and lay it above the high water line. Panting from exhaustion, they collapsed beside it on the warm sand.

Robbie pulled it further up on the sand and away from the incoming tide.

The woman uttered a soft moan. Astonished, Robbie jumped.

"Sweet mother of God! She's still alive! Quick Jamie, run for the wagon and my Elizabeth. She'll know what to do. You're faster than me, so I'll stay here."

Jamie stared at the woman in disbelief.

"She can't be alive Robbie."

Robbie placed his head on the woman's chest.

"She is. Now for the love of God man, hurry."

Jamie nodded his head, jumped up and ran as fast as the deep sand would allow him.

Robbie stared down at her. The storm had not been kind. Both eyes were swollen shut, while ugly welts and deep raw wounds crisscrossed her black and blue body.

Dusk was settling before he saw the rescue party approach. Jamie had returned with the wagon and some help. Elizabeth, sitting on the seat beside her brother-in-law, jumped down before it came to a complete stop. Kneeling, she ran gentle hands over the battered body.

Shaking her head, she whispered.

"Poor, poor lamb."

Two men pulled a sheet of canvas from the back of the wagon, laying it beside the un-conscious woman.

"Be careful with her."

Tears filled Elizabeth's dark brown eyes.

"I'll be surprised if she survives the journey back to the village. The poor little thing."

They placed her gently on the quilts and hay that covered the back of the wagon. The trip was slow and agonizing. Elizabeth tried her best to shield the woman from the jarring ride, but she could hear soft whimpers of pain as the wagon wheels bounced on the soft ruts in the sand.

At the end of the journey, they carried her into a little room next to the Tanner's kitchen and laid her on a cot. Elizabeth tried to make her patient comfortable. She bathed the young woman's wounds and covered them with salve. Robbie watched his wife as she tried to dribble a little cool water through parched, swollen lips.

Elizabeth sighed.

"It will be a miracle if she makes it through the night."

By next morning's light, the men went back to the shipwreck and gathered anything that was worth salvaging. The cape was still tangled in the rocks, but the tide had receded far enough that Robbie was able to walk out and hack the seaweed with his knife. The wet mass of wool was ripped and torn so badly that it was useless to save, but he solved one of the mysteries surrounding the wrecked ship. For there on the collar was embroidered the name, "Emma Hardwick".

Emma did survive the night and with Elizabeth's help she grew a little stronger each day. She never uttered a word for the harsh sea had stolen her will to speak.

One night, Robbie came in for supper after drying fish all day. Elizabeth placed his meal in front of him.

"I have news Robbie. Emma is with child."

Robbie whispered, afraid that Emma might hear from the next room.

"Is she strong enough?"

Elizabeth sat down across the table from her husband. Her clasped hands rested on the pine table.

"I don't know. Only the good Lord knows the answer to that."

Weeks went by and Emma slowly regained some of her strength. On stronger days she would take the path to the top of the dunes and stand searching the horizon.

Summer ebbed into fall. The swaying green grasses turned to a golden brown.

Now heavy with child, she still journeyed every day to the dunes and gazed out to sea. It almost broke Elizabeth's heart to watch the loneliness on her friend's face.

Late one fall night when the seas boiled and the winds whistled, Emma delivered her baby. She lived just long enough to hold her daughter to her breast. With sorrow etched on her face, she gazed down at her child and spoke for the last time.

"Anna."

The name issued forth in a sigh and with tears caressing her cheeks, she died.

Three hours later when the storm was at its peak, Anna closed her large blue eyes and followed her mother.

They buried them both together on the crest of the dunes with the babe cradled in her mother's arms. The villagers wept openly for Emma and her child, who had entered their hearts. She was a woman who had fought with the elements and won, only to have her life and that of her newborn child stolen from her.

Some will swear that when a raging storm subsides and the calm dawn ushers in a new day, you can see Emma standing on the crest of the dunes. Her black cape billowing in the still air, she stares out to sea watching and waiting with Anna in her arms.

ALL EYES WERE riveted on the stranger as he finished reading. A log snapped, splitting from the heat of the fire and rolled off the grate to the floor. Jumping up, the innkeeper grabbed an iron poker leaning against the stones of the fireplace. Pushing the burning wood back into the flames, he added another log.

Tipping his head back, the stranger drank the last of his ale. Placing the tankard on the table beside him, he sat upright on the bench easing his huge bulk in to some semblance of comfort. On the wide planked floor the movement of his hobnailed boots crushed the dried mud into a fine powder beneath his feet.

Orange flames flared and danced casting an erratic glow throughout their sanctuary from the storm. Thunder rattled overhead and rain beat against the windows. With great care, he turned another page and started to read as his voice rivaled the moaning wind.

The Peddler's Curse

"It's a fine home to bring a bride to."

Frederick Ramey stood with his hands on his hips and surveyed the lower level of the new Georgian house. Johann Conrad leaned against the wall of the vestibule in his new home nodding his head in agreement.

"You've done a fine job Frederick and I'm grateful. My Sarah Anne will be pleased."

The rattling of carriage wheels on the graveled drive interrupted their conversation. They looked out and watched as old Widow Whynacht climbed stiffly down from her carriage. She was dressed in black from head to toe. Gray strands of hair had escaped from the sides of her bonnet. A long strand of jet beads swung back and forth as she turned and faced the two men who were coming toward her.

Although both men were surprised to see her, they greeted her warmly.

She stood by the carriage, her face full of concern, ignoring their greetings.

"What in heavens name have you done Johann Conrad?"

Her shaky hands covered her blue veined cheeks. Her voice trembled with fear.

"Whatever have you done?"

Bewildered, the men stared at each other.

Johann tried to calm the agitated woman.

"I've built a new home. You're welcome to come in and see what Frederick and his men have built for me and Sarah Anne."

The widow vehemently shook her head.

"I'll not be crossing your doorway. This land is cursed."

She wrung her hands.

"If only I hadn't been so laid up this winter with my bones, I would have heard what you were doing and I could have stopped you."

Johann smiled indulgently at the old lady, for he was a kind man and didn't want to hurt her feelings.

"Those are just old wives tales."

The widow watched him, shaking her head.

"Years ago a house was built on this site and it burnt to the ground."

Johann looked at Frederick and winked.

"I know about the house, for I built my new one over part of the old foundation."

Frederick joined in the conversation.

"As sad as it was, these things are bound to happen."

He smiled at the old woman.

"So tell us. How did this land come to be cursed? "Come over and sit down under the apple tree and rest a spell."

Johann took her arm and helped her to the bench that lay almost covered with sweet scented blossoms. Frederick followed behind them with her cane. Her eyes darted back and forth across the homestead. They sensed her uneasiness.

"I won't be stoppin' here long. But I feel strongly you should know what you have to deal with."

She eased her body down on the bench and took her cane from Frederick, holding it with her gloved hands. Leaning forward painfully, she placed all her weight on the silver tipped cane. She eyed both of the men sitting on benches across from her as she cleared her throat.

"Years ago some folks came up from the colonies and settled on this here piece of land. Now the man, Thomas Baker was his name, had a black heart and he treated his wife and two daughters somethin' cruel, for he took to drink like a duck takes to the rushes along the water. Then late one day, toward dusk, an old peddler knocked on the kitchen door sellin' her laces and tellin' fortunes.

The old lady was hungry and asked for food in exchange for some of her laces. In a drunken rage, Thomas Baker shoved her off the stoop of the house where she fell to the rocky ground. He ranted and raved telling her he hated peddlers and to never set foot on his property again. Pickin' herself up, she limped down the lane to the road.

Not long after, Thomas hitched up his wagon for Lunenburg. He was makin' for the tavern with his hired hand in the wagon beside him. He two-wheeled it around the sharp bend of the road and came up on the old peddler. Aiming for her, he roared above the rattlin' of the wagon 'Good riddance you old hag, your end is near.' Terrified, the hired hand tried to pull the reins away from him, but Baker pushed him so hard that he fell off the wagon. The old lady was so frozen with fear that she couldn't move when the horses and wagon charged towards her. Then that beast of a man ran her down. Bleedin' and broken she lay crumpled in the dirt close to death. That monster pulled his horses to a stop and stood in his wagon laughin', like someone insane, at the poor dyin' woman. With her life ebbin' fast, she lifted her head from the blood soaked ground, pointed a crooked finger at Thomas Baker and dying, she cursed him.

'You'll not treat another soul as you've treated me. With my last breath, I curse the land that you live on. May it never see happiness again.' With one last rattle from her throat, deep crimson blood flowed from her lips. Then she died on the side of the dusty road, her vacant glassy eyes fixed on Thomas Baker."

Uncomfortable silence filled the air and then Frederick blustered.

"But that's just an old story. There was never a Baker that settled here."

The widow eyed him scornfully.

"Just a story is it?" Go check the land grant records. He bought this parcel of land from a Mingo."

Johann spoke quietly.

"So how is it cursed?"

The old lady pointed her cane toward the new house.

"Baker was found one week later hangin' from the floor joist in the cellar, shortly after that his wife and two daughters, begging and screamin' for help, burnt to death in a fire that leveled the house and barn to the ground."

She leaned closer to them and whispered.

"Forever wiping every trace of Thomas Baker and his family away."

Johann shook his head.

"That was very sad, but these things happen."

The widow snorted.

"Of course they do, but things don't keep happenin' on the same spot. Years later a small band of Micmacs camped right here because of the cove's good fishin'. They were found the next mornin', their throats cut. One of the men of the tribe murdered every man, woman and child who was sleepin'. Then he slit his own throat. They found the bloody knife still clenched in his hand."

With the aid of her cane, she pulled herself up and limped to where her horse pawed the ground. She climbed up into the carriage, with both men helping her to the seat.

"You're a good man Johann Conrad."

She reached down and touched him on the shoulder.

"Maybe that's what it takes to break the curse. If only I hadn't been laid up so, I might of been able to stop you."

Frederick put his hands through wide brown suspenders hoping to have the last word.

"How come you know so much about this curse?"

The widow looked down at both men.

"Because my grandfather was that hired hand."

She cracked her whip and the gray mare trotted smartly down the lane and through the wide opening of the gate.

A breeze stirred through the old apple tree. Tiny pink and white flowers drifted gently to the ground unnoticed, as the men stood together by the freshly painted fence watching her go.

Frederick clapped the younger man on the back, breaking the silence and grinned.

"Curse, my arse. That will be fodder for months at her afternoon tea parties. Where does she get off thinkin' she can scare two grown men with that old story about a curse. I think her last bout with sickness unhinged her a little bit...right?"

He gently nudged Johann in the ribs.

Johann finally smiled.

"You're right."

He unwrapped the reins of his horse from the brass hitching post and swung his leg over the agitated steed. Frederick calmed the spirited animal while Johann settled in the saddle.

He sensed that the widow's story upset the younger man more than he was admitting.

"The biggest thing you have to worry about is gettin' to the church in time to get hitched."

Johann pulled his horse around and started down the lane. He turned, waved and shouted.

"I'll be seein' you at the church Frederick."

The older man waved.

"I'll be there. You can count on it."

He stood there long after the horse and rider was out of sight, staring at the house with a somber look on his face.

The day of the wedding arrived, promising only as June days can, clear crisp mornings that mellow into still, sultry evenings.

Johann stood by the alter in St. John's Church looking out at their friends and family, waiting for Sarah Anne. Bright rays from the late morning sun danced through the stain glass windows, lighting up everything they touched, turning the house of worship into a kaleidoscope of color.

The organist began to play. The voices stilled with anticipation. Johann watched as the wide door at the back of the church opened and Sarah Anne entered with her father. Their eyes met and she smiled, taking his breath away. She was so lovely walking down the aisle, her arm through her father's, her head barely reaching his shoulder. Exquisite in her wedding gown of ivory silk, she reminded Johann of the porcelain dolls that were displayed in the shop windows of London.

He could hear the admiring whispers as she approached him. Her train flowed from the bow on the back of her tiny waist, rippling on the carpet like molten silk, as she passed each pew. Tiny pearl-encrusted roses covered the v-necked bodice and sleeves. Swaying softly against her shoulders, a floor length veil of lace gathered on a diamond and pearl comb. Matching pearl and diamond earrings, a gift from Johann, sparkled in the sun. She carried a cascading bouquet of white lilacs and lilies. Their soft scent perfumed the air as she moved.

Finally she was beside him, Johann covered her hand with his, clasping it to his heart. There in front of all their family and friends, he promised to love and cherish his Sarah Anne for the rest of his life.

After the wedding, a reception was held at their new home. The house was full to overflowing. Guests enjoyed no end of delicacies and drink and feasted for hours. All through the evening Frederick would find his wife, Margaret, standing uneasy by the main entrance of the house.

"What's wrong with you girl? Why don't you go in and have some fun with the rest of the womenfolk."

He smiled.

"Let me show you around the house. I think it's my best work yet."

Margaret shook her head, touched her husband's arm and whispered, her Scottish drawl soft in his ear.

"You'll think me crazy Freddy, but I'm stayin' close to the door. I den like the feel of this new home."

Frederick noticed the concern on his wife's face.

"What do you mean?"

Margaret sighed.

"It's like me ma and her ma before her."

She looked wearily at her husband.

"We can feel such things."

Frederick stared at his wife.

"You mean your gift?"

Margaret grimaced.

"A gift is it? I'd rather be callin' it a curse that the MacDonald women have to put up with. And I'm sorry to say that right now it's makin' me a wee bit ill."

Frederick looked at his wife's pale face and nodded his head.

"I'll get your wrap and say our good-byes to Johann. Then we'll head for home."

As he said goodbye to their host, the words of Widow Whynacht came back to haunt him and icy slivers ran through his blood.

Early the next morning, the newlyweds set sail for England on their honeymoon. Johann, being one of the youngest captains in Lunenburg to own his own vessel, was combining business with pleasure.

During their absence, Sarah Anne's parents were going to stay in the Georgian house while Frederick repaired their home.

Three months passed and just before they embarked for Lunenburg, Sarah Anne discovered that she was with child.

Johann held his wife tightly in his arms.

"Oh girl, you've made me the happiest man alive."

She hugged him, her face beaming with joy.

"I can hardly wait to see mama and papa's faces when they find out. They're going to be thrilled. They always wanted a big family and all they had was me."

Tenderly he kissed his wife.

"Maybe we'll have that big family for them."

Sarah Anne laughed up at her husband, tugging his chin.

"One at a time Johann Conrad."

For Sarah Anne, the return trip seemed to last forever. She missed her parents and wanted to see their faces when she told them about the happy event.

News had arrived in Lunenburg that the "Sarah Anne" was docking shortly.

Frederick waited on the busy wharf as Johann maneuvered his three-mast schooner alongside the mooring, with greater ease than many an older captain. He was the first to leave the ship and shouted with delight when he realized Frederick was waiting for him on the dock. However, his happiness was short lived when he caught the look of sorrow on his friend's face.

"There's somethin' wrong Frederick. I can see it in your eyes. Tell me what's wrong. What's happened?"

Frederick looked toward the ship hoping to tell his friend the horrendous news before Sarah Anne disembarked.

He placed his hand on Johann's shoulder.

"This is the hardest thing I've ever had to tell someone, but I must."

Johann's face drained of color. He could tell that the news was bad.

Frederick did not waste words.

"Johann, Sarah's parents are both dead."

His words stunned Johann.

"Dead! Both of them? How?"

Frederick rubbed his chin, shaking his head.

"The doctor thinks it was consumption, but he's not sure. He said he never saw anythin' like it."

Johann ran his hand through his hair.

"Consumption! They weren't even sick when we left. How can this be right? Archie Sarty never had a sick day in his life."

The cold reality of the situation washed over him as his wife walked down the gangplank, smiling and waving at them.

He closed his eyes. "Oh my God! How am I ever going to tell her? I just can't believe it. When did they die?"

"Yesterday mornin'. Archie went first and Sylvia died an hour later. The funeral is in two hours."

Johann pressed his fingers to his forehead. "Yesterday! Oh dear God Frederick, here she comes. What am I going to say? I just can't believe it."

Sarah walked towards them and smiled, only hearing the last sentence her husband uttered to Frederick.

"Believe what?"

She laughed.

"Oh Johann, you just couldn't wait to tell Frederick our wonderful news. That's just like a..."

She stopped speaking as she gazed into the faces of both men.

"What's wrong Johann?"

She watched her husband's eyes fill with tears.

Cold fear, like icy hands, seized her heart.

He reached for his wife and gently pulled her into the protection of his arms. Her eyes searched his, asking, but not wanting answers.

He stroked her face and hair.

"I'm so sorry Sarah Anne."

His voice raw with emotion, he sighed deeply, tears pooling at the corners of his eyes. He spoke almost in a whisper.

"Your mother and father are dead. They're being buried today."

For seconds, she seemed frozen, hardly able to take in the horrible news. Finally the reality of his words seared her consciousness and she screamed against his chest, while he tried to console her.

"No! No! Please God tell me it isn't true!"

With tears streaming down her face, she pleaded with Frederick.

"I have to see them. Where are they?"

Johann's eyes locked with Frederick's and the older man shook his head.

"The coffins are closed my dear. We thought it best. Come home with me. My Margaret is waitin' for you."

Two hours later, in Hillcrest Cemetery, with her husband's arms around her, she stood at the foot of the black yawning hole that would soon be the last resting place for her parents' wasted bodies. In a flutter of wings, she had lost both of them, never knowing her joyous news, never saying good-bye.

Numb she stared, with eyes blinded by grief, at the water in Lunenburg's back harbor. As if keeping time to a silent funeral drum, a gray bank of fog slowly crept in, weeping its mist over the last rites. Reverend Cochrane's words reverberated against the moist blanket that enveloped the place of mourning.

"We therefore commit these bodies to the grave. Earth to earth, ashes to ashes, dust to dust."

As the first thud of earth hit the oak coffins, she screamed.

"Momma! Papa! Don't leave me! Momma I need you!"

Bolting from Johann's comforting arms, she ran sobbing to the open abyss, trying to throw herself on the coffins. Grabbing Sarah Anne, he pulled her back. Half crazed, she struggled with him in front of family and friends before crumpling by the side of her parents' grave.

Terrified, he pleaded with Frederick.

"Help me! Help me with Sarah Anne."

They took her home. Johann carried his wife up the sweeping stairs and laid her on their bed. Hired nurses cared for his unconscious Sarah Anne day and night, the weeks slipping by. She lay in a coma, her life and the life of their unborn child dangling by a fragile thread.

One day, late in November, Margaret stood on the curved brick steps watching her husband and Johann ride up the lane. Johann darted from the wagon and ran up the steps to where she stood.

"What is it? Is it Sarah Anne?"

Margaret took him by the arms.

"She's awake Johann. She's askin' for you. Go to her."

He ran up the wide stairway, taking two steps at a time, until he reached his wife's sick room.

Throwing back the door, he rushed to his wife's bedside kneeling close to her.

"Oh Johann, what happened?"

Her weak voice barely a whisper.

"What's wrong with me?"

He took her hand and held it to his lips.

"You've been very ill, but now you're gonna get better."

She looked at him afraid to ask the question that stayed on her lips. She swallowed imploring him with her eyes. Finally she said.

"And our baby?"

He nodded, his hand touching her stomach gently.

"You still carry our child and now every day you'll get stronger."

Her beautiful blue eyes that sparkled with such joy on her wedding day, lay dull and sunken in her wasted, pale face as she tried to smile at him.

Over the next weeks her strength slowly returned. For a short time each day, she was able to sit by the fire in her room, read or knit tiny garments in soft wool. She had no desire for food, but she forced herself to eat for her unborn child.

A few days before Christmas, Frederick and his wife stopped for a visit. Margaret wanted to give Sarah Anne a tonic, a recipe that had been passed down through her family for generations. She sat and watched the young woman, hardly more than a skeleton, rock slowly in her chair staring at the glass bottle in her hand. Margaret tried to keep her voice light and cherry, but it was so hard when her heart was breaking.

"You take this three times a day Sarah Anne, morning, noon and night. It will build up your strength for the wee bairn and put some roses back into those pretty cheeks of yours. It got me through all five of my confinements and everyone round these parts always says that Frederick Ramey has five strappin' big lads."

As they drove away, Margaret took her husband's arm.

"Stay close to home Frederick, that poor man is going to need you soon."

He stared at his wife.

"Why do you say that?"

She shook her head.

"I'm afraid that's the last time we'll see Sarah Anne alive."

Christmas Eve day arrived bright and cold. Earlier that morning a soft blanket of snow had covered the ground. Sophia, the little maid, entered her mistress's room to build up the coals in the fireplace and discovered that Sarah Anne was missing. She ran to Johann's room, pounding on the door with both hands.

"Mr. Conrad! Mr. Conrad! Come quickly! She's gone!"

The search covered every corner of every room in the house. Sarah Anne was not to be found.

Johann stood in the middle of the large empty attic, his footsteps echoing on the rough bare boards. He knew he wouldn't find her there, but it was his last hope. He placed his hands over his face and prayed.

"Oh Sarah Anne, please be okay."

Sophia shouted from the bottom of the attic steps.

"Mr. Conrad! The kitchen door, it's open!"

He ran to the kitchen. Sophia and Angus, his hired hand, were staring at the snow-covered stoop on the back porch.

He moaned.

"Oh dear God...no!"

Sophie pulled the skirt of her apron up to her face sobbing,

"She's left in her bare feet. Why Mr. Conrad? Why?"

Johann grabbed his coat and boots. He turned and yelled.

"Angus, ride to Frederick's. Tell him we need him and his men. "Tell him..."

Tears streamed down his face.

"Tell him my Sarah Anne is missin'."

Angus MacDonald ran to the barn as fast as he could, knowing even before he threw his leg over the saddle that help would be too late in coming.

Early Christmas morning when the church bells of Lunenburg rang out, rejoicing the glad tidings of the day, Johann pulled his wife's cold, stiff body from the well. The men watched in silence as he carried her into the house, holding his Sarah Anne to his heart for the very last time.

He buried her next to her parents, overlooking the back harbor. Two angels, with marble tears streaming down their faces, comfort each other, marking the grave where Sarah Anne lay with their unborn child.

One week to the day after they said goodbye to Sarah Anne, Frederick loosened the noose from the neck of Johann's lifeless body. Easing it from the large beam, he laid him on the floor of the cellar. Kneeling over his friend he sobbed.

"Why Johann? Why?"

Fire roared and danced in the cold night. Frederick watched as the roof of the Georgian house collapsed, shooting flames out through the second story windows. Orange and blue tongues of fire licked the wood consuming it. Leaving in ashes, not only the house, but also the dreams and desires of those who had once lived there.

Satisfied, he watched as the walls collapsed, falling in on each other. Huge billowing clouds of smoke circled back and forth before being pushed into the cove by a screeching wind.

Breathing in deeply, the smoke seared his aching lungs. He clenched his fist and screamed.

"Johann, I swear to you tonight, for as long as I live that I'll never let any man own this land again. That's my promise to you."

After a final silent farewell to his friend, he turned and walked away, leaving the howling wind and the last of the shooting flames to mourn without him.

THE THUNDER WAS moving away, but lightening still danced through the night sky. Rain drummed on the roof as the stranger finished reading.

Turning the next page, he folded his hands over the book and stared intently at his tankard.

The innkeeper rose from the bench. Collecting the empty tankard and lantern, he carried them to the bar. He opened the glass door of the lantern. Replacing the candle and filling the mug to the rim, he sat them down by the stranger's side.

"Read on my friend. The night is long and the storm still rages outside."

The stranger nodded and drank. His captive audience waited with baited breath as he turned the next page.

The House on the Hill

"What's in the basket Becky?"

Bert Veinotte leaned against the kitchen table and pulled at the checkered cloth that covered the large wicker basket. Rebecca finished placing more wood in the stove, marched over and slapped her brother's hands before he could upset the contents of the basket all over the table.

"Ouch! What did you go and do that for? I was only lookin'."

He grinned down at her from his six foot two height.

Becky tipped her neck back and pointed her finger; her head barely reaching his shoulder.

"Because there's food in the basket and it's not safe around you."

With very little effort, he picked her up by the waist and placed her on the other side of the table. She tried to wiggle out of his grip, but his large callused hands completely encircled her middle.

She slapped both his hands.

"I hate it when you do that."

Bert grinned.

"I know and that's why I do it."

She gave him a push and then stood in front of the basket.

"Is that any way to treat your older brother?" I need food."

She dug him in the ribs.

"You're only one hour older."

Elsie Veinotte entered the kitchen and stood watching her children from the doorway. They were like two peas in a pod. Becky wore her tightly curled hair knotted on the crown of her head. Soft strands had escaped the confines of the knot and floated around her face and the nape of her neck forming tiny ringlets. Her green eyes danced with laughter as she teased her twin brother. Bert, his face clean-shaven, had the exact coloring. His sister had stopped growing at five foot two, but he had kept growing 'til be towered over the womenfolk of the family.

Becky noticed her mother standing in the doorway.

"Ma, will you tell Bert to leave the basket alone?"

Elsie smiled at both of them, shaking her head.

"Bert, leave the basket alone, it's not for you. I swear you two have been bickering since before you were born and you're still at it twenty-three years later."

Becky removed her apron and placed it on the hook behind the stove.

"Well he's always starting it."

She picked up her straw hat from the cot in the corner and stood in front of the oval mirror. She teased Bert with her sharp hatpin before pushing it through her hat. With a flourish, she tied the ribbon into a wide bow under her chin.

He pulled a chair out from the table and settled his long legs over it. Crossing his arms, he surveyed her from head to toe taking in the calico dress of mint green. Delicate pink flowers covered the mutton sleeve bodice and high neckline. Polished black boots peeped out from under the full flowered skirt.

"You know Becky, you look just like a school marm."

She pulled a towel from over the sink and threw it at her brother.

"Maybe that's because I am one."

Taking the wicker basket by the smooth wooden handles, she pulled them over her arm.

"You still haven't told me where you're going dressed like that this time of day."

Standing in front of him, she pulled his red curly hair.

"New folks from away have moved to the house on the hill and I'm going to make a welcome visit. I'll be back after a spell."

She waved to them as the screen door banged behind her.

Elsie walked around the corner to the pantry and carried back a tray of barley bread, pickles, cheese and a crock of butter. She placed it on the table across from her son.

"I reckon I'd better make you a sandwich. I'll not have enough to go around the table tonight, if you don't eat before supper time."

Turning to the counter, she removed a knife hanging on the wall. Shaking her head, Elsie smiled at her son.

"I swear I don't know where you put it."

He watched as his mother made his cheese and pickle sandwich.

"I'm still a growing boy Ma."

She placed the food in front of him ruffling his hair.

Well you can stop any time. Here now eat this and tell me what you've been up to."

Bert wolfed down the sandwich.

"Me and Gus just finished cutting the rest of the logs."

He snorted.

"I should have told Becky that I was cutting the wood for her new house. She might have been nicer to me."

They were interrupted by the appearance of Elsie's mother. Eyes twinkling, she watched her daughter cleaning off the table. She grinned and walked over to the high back rocker on the other side of the stove.

"Are you feedin' this boy again? It's time he got himself a wife."

The old lady shook her head looking around the room.

"Where's our Becky?"

Bert swallowed and answered before his mother had a chance to.

"She's gone callin' on the new people who have moved into the house on the hill."

She stopped rocking and stared at her grandson.

"There are people moved in there again? Who are they?"

Elsie went to the sink and pushed the handle of the pump up and down a few times before water flowed out. She filled a large enamel cup to the brim and placed it in front of Bert.

He shrugged his shoulders and looked across at his mother who stood by the stove pouring two saucers of tea.

"Did Becky tell you Ma?"

Elsie passed a saucer to her mother and sat down next to Bert, nodding her head.

"Robert Langille told her on the last day of school when she was getting paid. It's some barrister from Halifax and his widowed daughter."

The old lady blew on her hot tea and took a sip.

"It's been a long time since there's been people livin' in that house. They won't stay there long, they never do. It's been standin' empty a good many years."

Elsie reached over to the middle of the table and pulled a covered cake plate in front of her. She removed the round tin dome and the smell of spicy molasses cake filled the kitchen. Taking the knife, she cut three generous slices of the moist fragrant cake and passed it to her mother and son before sitting down.

"Who built the place Nana?"

Elsie pulled a piece of the cake apart, popping it into her mouth.

Nana rocked back and forth.

"I don't know or if I did I've forgotten. That old house has been here in Blockhouse not long after Lawrence landed at Rouses' Brook and settled

Lunenburg. Now the house has changed over the years. Every time it changed hands, folks would fix it up differently."

The old lady drank her tea, deep in thought.

"I think my pa said an Obediah Hebb owned it for a long time. He had a wife and daughter, but they didn't mingle much with the folks around these parts. My pa told me old Obediah was too full of religious zeal."

She took another sip of the hot tea and rocked, her feet barely touching the floor.

"I guess he didn't think a soul should have a little fun cause his womenfolk weren't allowed to join in on nothin'. Then when the daughter was marryin' age, I guess my pa tried to go a courtin' cause he said she was a pretty thing, but old Obediah told him that her and her ma had left. Her and her ma had to leave for a spell and nurse a sick relative. Well my pa said about two months after they left, Obediah was found dead in his bed. He said it was the strangest thing he ever saw. He said that his bed and floor was covered with dried up dead lilacs."

Nana placed the empty saucer on the corner of the wood box.

"There was no way to reach the wife and daughter cause no one knew where they came from and didn't know any of the relatives. And they never came back. A couple of years passed and

Sheriff Kaulback went and sold the house. People would settle in and then it would be empty again. Like I said, they didn't stay long."

Elsie got up and moved over to the stove and opened the oven door. Using the hem of her apron, she pulled a large brown crock of baked beans and pork from the oven stirring them with a wooden spoon. Removing two pans of barley bread, she pushed the oven shut with her hip. Placing the bread on the back of the stove, Elsie wiped her flushed face with her apron.

"Well Nana, maybe it will be different this time."

Twenty minutes after Becky said her good-byes, she pulled the heavy brass knocker with her free hand and banged it against the door three times. Moments later, she heard muffled footsteps coming toward her from inside. A tall willowy young woman flung the door back.

"Yes, can I help you?"

Gleaming sable hair was swept up from the sides of her heart shaped face knotting on the top of her head. A gold cameo was pinned at the base of her lace-covered throat. She wore matching cameos on her ears. A long full skirt of navy linen fell in folds from a tiny waist. Sparkling brown eyes smiled at her, waiting for an answer.

Becky, suddenly feeling very self-conscious, stood in her homemade garment facing this beautiful young woman dressed from the best shops in Halifax.

She fumbled over her words.

"Hello, my name...my name is Rebecca Veinotte and I thought you might be able to use this since you'd be too busy movin' in to make somethin'."

"Oh my, how nice of you. I'm Laura Wile. Please come in and have tea with me."

Becky took the handles of the basket and passed it to her. By now she was glad to get rid of the heavy load. Laura placed it on a three-legged table by the door and pulled off the cloth, looking inside.

"Oh, how thoughtful."

Becky went over to the basket and took out a jar.

"These are Ma's baked beans and there's barley bread."

Laura pulled out a cloth-covered plate. She leaned over and took a deep breath.

"What is this wonderful smell?"

Becky smiled.

"That's my ma's famous molasses spice cake."

Laura smelled it again and laughed.

"This is what we're having for tea."

She placed everything back into the basket and took Becky by the arm.

"Why don't you sit in the parlor and I'll put the kettle on."

She led Becky to the room on the right, just inside the front door.

It was a lovely room, with double windows overlooking the road. A single window on the right wall allowed sunlight to shimmer on the wine carpet lying on the floor. A wide pine mantle, draped with lace dollies, crowned the fireplace on the end wall. Waiting invitingly, a camel back sofa stood in front of the double windows. Lace drapes danced and whirled against the back of a love seat. A charming oil painting of a much younger Laura and an older woman hung over the mantle; the ornate gilded frame almost touching the dentine plaster molding of the ceiling.

Becky was standing in front of the portrait when Laura entered the parlor carrying a tray with a silver teapot and china cups and saucers. She placed the tray on a small side table by the sofa.

"Here we are, afternoon tea."

She poured the golden liquid and raised her eyebrows at Becky as she held the little silver jug full of milk over the teacup. Becky smiled and nodded her head.

"Just a little please."

Over afternoon tea, the young women came to know each other very well. Although from different backgrounds, they were fast becoming friends.

The ornate French clock on a side table chimed three times. Becky jumped up from her chair.

"Oh my goodness Laura, I've been talkin' your head off for more than an hour. I expect you have a lot to do and here I am sitting when I should have offered to help you."

Laura smiled, shaking her head.

"I've enjoyed every minute of it. Father has gone to Halifax again and won't be back till the first of the month. Mrs. Wambolt and her sister, Mrs. Romkey, have been here most of the week helping so I'm as settled as I'll ever be."

Becky stood up and walked to the front door with Laura behind her.

"Laura?"

Becky hesitated.

"Gus and I are going on a picnic tomorrow afternoon. Would you like to go with?"

Laura's eyes lit up.

"That sounds wonderful."

Then her smile faded.

"Oh, are you sure Becky? You don't want me tagging along."

"Of course I'm sure. When Gus talks about a picnic, it means bring as much food as you can

50

carry and I'll do some fishing after I'm done eatin'. I'll bring my brother, Bert, along and he can keep Gus company while we visit with each other."

Laura touched Becky's arm. Her voice was still hesitant.

"Well, if you're sure."

Becky smiled.

"Of course I'm sure."

"Then, I want to bring something for the picnic."

"Bring whatever you want to. Bert is just like Gus. The more food the better the picnic is."

They stood on the front steps.

"We'll stop for you here, mid mornin'."

Both women said goodbye and Laura, standing on the stoop, waved until her new friend was out of sight.

Becky walked toward home with a light heart for she knew that she had found a kindred spirit.

Sunday morning dawned warm and clear, a perfect day for a picnic. Gus's wagon stopped in front of Laura's house and Becky was amused at how tongue tied her otherwise vocal twin was.

Spring wafted into summer. The girls had become fast friends. One hot day they sat in the shade of an apple tree in the Veinotte orchard.

"Laura? I don't know how to ask you this, so I'm gonna come right out with it."

Laura alarmed by the concern on Becky's face.

"What is it Becky?"

Becky sighed.

"I would like you to...mm I mean, ah...oh dear, what I'm tryin' to say is, would you like to stand with me at my weddin'?"

Laura hugged Becky, tears of laughter running down her face.

"I'd love to Becky."

Two weeks after Becky's first meeting with Laura, she was introduced to Mr. Emeneau. He was a kind, quiet man who clearly adored his daughter. A barrister, he practiced law in Halifax until he retired, selling his business to a younger partner. Tired of the busy life, he yearned for a more peaceful existence. The city carried sad memories for both of them. He lost his wife to consumption. Shortly after that, Laura lost her husband of only two weeks in a tragic fire.

One day after a visit with Laura, Mr. Emeneau walked Becky to the door.

"I want to thank you Miss Veinotte for all you've done to make Laura welcome. She's like her old self. The death of her husband has been hard for her to deal with, even though it was almost five years ago."

Becky smiled.

"She is a true friend and I'm glad I found her."

Close to one o'clock in the morning, the Veinotte's heard pounding on their kitchen door. Bert, pulling his pants on, reached the door first only to have Laura collapse in his arms.

"Oh Bert come quick, there's something wrong with father. Please hurry. I don't know what to do. I heard him calling for help, but his bedroom door was locked and I couldn't get in. Please hurry. I'm so afraid."

When they reached the house they ran into Mr. Emeneau's bedroom. They found his lifeless body curled up on the floor in the corner, his hands bloody and torn. Large chunks of broken plaster covered the floor around him. Filled with horror, his vacant eyes stared past them.

The day of the funeral arrived and Mr. Emeneau's body lay in the parlor waiting to be transported to the church. The closed coffin sat on a black crepe covered table under the mantel. Two large vases of June roses, that Becky and her mother had picked that morning, stood on either side of the fireplace.

Elsie sat beside Laura and held her hands.

"What are you going to do now my dear? Close the house up and go back to Halifax?"

Laura shook her head. Her eyes, puffy and red, started to fill with fresh tears.

"I'm staying here. I've made friends and I need to settle down. I don't have the energy to move again and I like this village."

She gave Elsie a watery smile.

"And I like the people. They've been very kind and friendly."

Reverend Owen entered the room searching for Laura.

"Are you ready, my dear?"

Laura nodded her head and Becky took her cold hand and squeezed it gently.

"Let us pray."

As he started to pray over the coffin, the six pallbearers entered and took their place on either side of the table with Bert and Gus standing at the head of the coffin. As the prayers were ending, they picked the coffin up by the brass handles and followed Reverend Owen as he loudly read more exerts from the prayer book for the burial of the dead. Carefully, they maneuvered their heavy burden through the hall and out the open door. Laura followed behind her father's coffin with Becky and Elsie walking beside her. The rest of the community quietly waited outside as the coffin was carried down the front steps of the house. They watched as it was pushed into the glass sided carriage hearse.

A soft warm breeze ruffled the black plumes on the horse's harness. Old German hymns softly filled the air, as the people of Blockhouse marched solemnly behind the hearse to the church and her father's final resting place.

After the funeral, the Veinotte's helped ease the sorrow and loneliness that followed in the wake of Mr. Emeneau's untimely death. Bert and Laura began seeing a lot of each other and the four young people were constantly together.

July eased into August. Hot, breathless days melted into long, sultry evenings. The kind of evenings that were suited for rocking on the verandah, taking long walks through clover scented pastures before dallying on the moss covered banks of a gurgling brook.

It was one such evening that Bert invited Laura to go walking to the upper pasture. He sprinted up the hill ahead of her.

"Wait a minute Laura and I'll open the gate for you." She nodded and waited until he pushed the heavy gate aside. They stood leaning against the fence looking down on the farmhouse.

He closed his eyes and took a deep breath.

"It's a good place to live, isn't it Laura?"

Waiting for her to answer, he leaned over and pulled out a long stem of the sweet hay, sticking it between his teeth.

Their eyes met and she smiled.

"It's a wonderful place to live Bert."

"You know Laura, there was a time when I went up to Dalhousie to be a doctor, but six months after I settled in, Pa got sick and then died."

She slid her arm through his and squeezed his hand. Her face filled with sympathy as she gazed at his handsome profile.

"I'm so sorry Bert, I never knew. How long ago did this happen?"

"It's almost four years now. I put away my books and came home right away to take over the farm. I never had a pang of regret. I guess this is where I really belong. Its hard work, but I can make a good livin'. I can't think of anywhere else I'd rather see my children grow."

Bert's gaze traveled across the gated pasture down to the sprawling farmhouse in the hollow below. Fat pink clouds hovered over the horizon heralding the exodus of the sun.

He chewed on the grass, wondering how to begin. Clearing his throat, Bert tried to remember the speech he had painstakingly prepared earlier that day.

"I know that, uh we uh haven't known each other for a long time and I know that you've had more sorrow than you deserve, but...if you could see yourself clear to stay here...and be my wife, I'd try to keep you happy 'til your dyin' day."

He heard Laura give a tiny gasp and then silence. To Bert it seemed to go on forever.

He broke the stillness that lay between them; not daring to gaze into her eyes, so afraid of what he would read. Bert tried to swallow, but his mouth felt as dry as the thrashing floor at harvest time.

"I'm sorry Laura."

He spoke to the gatepost. The single piece of grass lay crushed in his large hands.

"I didn't mean to take you unaware. You don't have to give me an answer now."

He drew all the courage he had, stood his full height and looked down into the face of the woman he loved.

"But please say yes Laura."

He begged softly.

Two silent tears escaped from deep brown limpid pools and trickled down her radiant face.

"Oh yes, Bert. Yes! I would be proud to be your wife."

There in the dusky pasture with the crickets shrilling, he pulled Laura into his arms and sealed his pledge with a kiss.

The Veinotte's were delighted with the news. Laura and Bert sat on the verandah, while Gus kept clapping Bert on the back and grinning. Becky sat on the railing across from them. Leaning over, she gave Laura a hug.

"I'm finally getting a sister. I can't believe that this big lug asked you to marry him. Have you set the time? Is it going to be soon?"

Laura laughed trying to answer Becky's questions in order.

"We thought we'd wait 'till spring. This year is for you and Gus."

Nana, rocking in her favorite chair, stopped knitting and nodded her head.

"That's fair. A person can only handle one weddin' at a time."

One morning, a few days later, Becky knocked on Laura's front door. She waited for a few moments and then knocked again, but no one answered. She thought this strange because Laura was expecting her.

She walked around the path to the kitchen door and knocked again, calling out.

"Laura, are you in there? It's me, Becky."

She pulled up on the latch and the wooden plank door opened. Moving through the wood room, she entered the kitchen.

"Laura? Laura? Where are..."

Becky raised her hands to her face and shrieked.

"Oh my soul in heaven."

Laura, still in her nightclothes, lay sprawled by the door to the front hall. Her ashen face crusted with blood. More blood lay congealing by her head. A plait of hair lay to the side of her head, soaked.

Becky ran to Laura.

"Oh mercy, mercy, mercy."

She shook her gently.

"Laura?"

Getting no response, she slapped her hand shouting.

"Laura? Answer me."

Laura's eyes opened. Deep blue and purple bruises covered most of the left side of her face. Both cheeks were covered in blood. Becky held her breath as she leaned over examining the wound on Laura's head. She mumbled a small prayer when the bleeding seemed to have stopped.

Laura tried to focus.

"Becky?"

She moaned.

"Ohhhh, my head hurts."

"What happened Laura?"

Laura tried to remember, her eyes blurring with pain.

"I don't know!" She tried to move, but it was almost unbearable.

Becky jumped up.

"I've got to get help! Maybe I can run for..."

"Listen Laura!"

Becky heard the rattling of wagon wheels on the road in front of the house.

She ran to the front door and pulled it open just in time to see the end of George Joudrey's wagon bouncing down the road.

Pulling her long, full skirt up to her knees, she raced out the door and down the front walk as fast as her legs would carry her, shouting at the top of her voice.

"Mr. Joudrey stop! Stop Mr. Joudrey!"

She ran holding up her skirt and apron. Her lungs bursting for air, she passed the horse and wagon. Stopping in the middle of the road she waved her arms frantically.

Flabbergasted at the sight in front of him, George Joudrey pulled back hard on the reins.

"Whoa there! Whooaa!"

He stared at Becky in astonishment, shouting.

"What in tarnation are you trying to do girl? Get yourself killed?"

Becky leaned over, gasping for air.

"I'm sorry Mr. Joudrey, but Laura Wile has had a bad accident. Could you please go get my ma and bring her here? We need her bad. I'd go for her, but I'm afraid to leave Laura by herself."

After Becky's faltering speech, Mr. Joudrey leapt into action. He had his wagon and horse turned around before she could move to the side of the road. Snapping the reins, the wagon rattled down the road in a cloud of dust.

She ran back to the house and knelt on the kitchen floor beside Laura.

"The good Lord must be lookin' down on us because that was Mr. Joudrey and he went to fetch Ma."

She removed her shawl and tucked it around Laura's body.

"I'd better not move you 'til she gets here."

Laura faded in and out of consciousness. Finally, after what seemed like hours, Becky heard the rumble of a wagon.

"Becky? Where are you girl?"

"In here, Ma. We're in the kitchen."

Entering the room, Elsie gasped when she saw Laura sprawled on the floor. Kneeling on the other side of the girl, she touched her head gently.

"What happened child?"

Laura moved her head slightly but grimaced, as pain shot through it.

"I don't know."

She whispered.

"I had just gone to bed and decided to read when I thought I heard a noise down here. I came down to check. I felt a draft and thought..."

Laura stopped, licked her dry lips and looked imploring at Becky.

"Becky, could I have some water?"

Becky nodded her head, rose quickly and went to the pump. Pushing it hard, she filled a glass that stood by the sink. She passed it to her mother and between them they gently propped Laura up as she sipped the cool refreshing liquid. Revived a little, she closed her eyes to clear the pain before continuing with her story.

"The air felt cold and damp. I thought that maybe I had left the kitchen window open."

Tears of pain ran down her face creating small channels on her blood-encrusted cheeks.

"I can't remember much after I entered the kitchen except how cold it was. I guess I must have tripped on my dressing gown and hit my head on the rocking chair."

The rocking chair, which usually stood inside the kitchen door from the hall, now lay on its side.

Elsie pursed her lips, shaking her head.

"Well you have one nasty wound. The only place for you is bed. Becky, help me pick her up and ..."

At that moment, the front door was thrown open and they heard footsteps thundering down the hall.

"Laura? Laura?"

Bert stood in the doorway, his face turning pale as he saw all the blood on the floor.

"Oh dear God! Is she okay, Ma?"

Laura tried to smile.

"I'm fine, Bert."

Elsie patted her son's shoulder as he knelt beside her.

"She's going to be all right. She needs to take to her bed for a spell."

Bert questioned his mother.

"But ma, look at all the blood."

"Now don't fret so. Be a good lad and carry her up to her room."

Bert lifted Laura gently, treating her as if she were made of bubbles and stardust.

When they were all in Laura's room, Elsie shooed him away.

"Now she's goin' to be fine, but she needs her rest. She's lost a lot of blood. Becky's gonna stay and nurse her.

Elsie looked at her son's face and took pity on him.

"You can come round after supper to visit for a bit. Promise me you won't stay long, for she's lost a lot of blood and she needs her rest."

After giving his word, Bert left. Leaving his mother and sister to care for Laura.

Elsie removed a small paper envelope from her covered basket and tipped the contents into a glass of water.

"This will ease the pain and help you get some sleep."

They supported Laura while Elsie held the glass to her lips. After drinking the medication, she sank back into the pillows, whispering as her eyes fluttered shut.

Laura whispered

"Thank-you Mrs. Veinotte."

"You're welcome child and you may as well call me Ma, like the rest of my brood."

Laura smiled; sleep already overtaking her.

"Thanks, Ma."

Becky and Elsie tiptoed quietly from the sickroom and down to the kitchen.

"I'll send Bert over with some clothes for you dear. It's no tellin' how long you're gonna' stay. She's weak cause she's lost a lot of blood, but I've seen a lot worse. Keep a close eye on her."

Elsie stared at the rocking chair still on its side in the corner, shaking her head perplexed.

"I just can't understand how she could get such nasty wounds by trippin' on that rocking chair."

She straightened the chair and waved to Becky as she walked to the front door.

Becky spent the rest of the day scrubbing the blood from the kitchen floor and making a nourishing meal for her patient.

True to his word, Bert arrived shortly after supper holding a wicker basket and a cloth bag. A bouquet of wild flowers, in brilliant colors, peeked over the rim.

"Ma sent some food."

He waved the cloth bag in the air.

"And here's some clothes for ya."

Dropping the bag carelessly to the floor, he glanced up at the ceiling.

"Is Laura awake?"

Becky grinned.

"Yes she is and even if she wasn't, I know you'd wake her. She's been waiting for you."

She shook her finger at him.

"But you can't stay long or Ma will have my head."

Bert scooped the flowers from the top of the basket and ran up the stairs. He poked his head around the door of Laura's room.

"Are you feelin' better girl? I picked you some flowers."

He held out the bouquet of slightly wilted wild flowers that he had picked on the way over. Searching the room, he eyed the pitcher of water on Laura's bedside table. After sticking the flowers in the water, he dragged a wingback chair close to her bed.

Laura smiled weakly.

"Oh Bert, thank-you, they're lovely."

Sitting down he cupped her hand in his.

"You scared the hell out of me girl. There you were lyin' on the floor covered with blood, your face white as a newborn lamb. It took ten years from me. Can you remember what happened?"

Laura tried to shake her head, wincing as pain shot through it.

"I'm still not sure what happened. I guess I'll never know. It just happened."

Laura's dark eyelashes fluttered. Bert could tell that she was fighting to stay awake. Smiling, he leaned over and kissed her cheek and tiptoed toward the door.

She whispered.

"Thank-you for the lilacs."

Bert glanced over to the bouquet of wild flowers. Strange, he thought, they do smell like lilacs.

A few days passed and Laura was almost back to her old self. Elsie thought that Becky should stay with her for a few more days just to make sure that she had recovered.

They were sitting in the parlor relaxing. The evening was damp and dismal, but a cozy fire snapped and crackled in the open grate. Becky hemmed the skirt of her wedding gown while Laura reclined on the settee watching her. Yards of soft cream satin covered her lap. Flowing to the floor, it encircled her chair. Firelight shimmered and danced on the material causing her gown to glow with a life of its own.

Laura sighed, watching Becky's skillful use of the needle.

"Your gown is going to be so lovely Becky. You're a wonderful seamstress."

Becky snorted disgusted.

"Maybe, but I don't have the sense to come in out of the rain."

She shook her head and sighed deeply.

"Why I thought I had to embroider tiny rose buds on my bodice and all along the hem is somethin' I will never be able to answer."

Laura laughed at Becky's screwed up face.

"I'll tell you why. Because it's going to be absolutely gorgeous."

Becky rolled her eyes.

"Then it'll be your job to keep remindin' me 'til I finish it. Okay?"

Laura nodded her head.

"Okay, I promise."

They were interrupted by the sound of a wagon rattling to a stop. Becky jumped up, causing the gown to puddle at her feet.

"It's Gus and Bert."

She looked at Laura.

"What are they doin' here tonight?"

The knocker banged against the door.

Becky bent down and scooped her gown up into her arms.

"I'll put this away and you answer the door."

By the time she returned to the parlor, Bert and Gus were sitting on either side of the fireplace.

Gus jumped up and gave Becky an embarrassed hug.

"I missed you girl. Bert and I thought we'd surprise you with a visit."

Laura watched Becky blush, red freckles shining on the bridge of her nose. They made an attractive couple, Gus with his dark good looks against Becky's striking red coloring. It was obvious that he adored her.

Becky pulled at the bottom of Gus's chin, scolding.

"Augustus Zinck, you almost saw my wedding dress."

He smiled down at her.

"I can hardly wait to see you comin' toward me in it. The Banns are going to be called this Sunday, so there's no turnin' back now girl."

Bert sat beside Laura beaming at his lifelong friend and sister.

"I've waited all my life to get rid of this one. I'll make sure she gets to the church Gus. Don't you worry."

She crossed her arms and pouted.

"I was gonna offer you some cake with rhubarb preserves, but after the way you let your mouth run away with you, you can forget it."

Later Gus and Bert left after having two helpings of cake.

Laura and Becky gathered up the dishes and took them to the pantry to wash.

"Laura, do you know where you and Bert are gonna live?"

Laura thought for a moment before answering.

"We haven't discussed it very much yet. Maybe sell this place and move to the farm. It would be easier for Bert."

Becky put the last of the pink Spode dessert set carefully on the shelf.

"These are so pretty, it's almost a shame to put food on them."

Laura nodded.

"I love them. They belonged to my mother and wherever I live they'll go with me."

"Well, I wouldn't worry about it just yet, you have a whole year to think about it."

She picked up the oil lamp from the kitchen observing Laura's pale face.

"I think it's time we went to bed. You're still not right from your fall and Ma will have my head if you don't get your proper rest."

A few hours later, Becky was awaken from a deep sleep by what she thought was a severe thunderstorm. Sitting up, she discovered her bedroom was bathed in a soft golden glow from the full moon shining high in the clear night sky.

The sound of Laura screaming her name scattered the last dregs of sleep from her unconsciousness.

"Becky! Becky! Wake up. What's happening?"

She jumped out of bed and ran into Laura's room. The ominous clamor of glass breaking and furniture smashing against the kitchen walls reverberated through the house. They clung to each other for support.

"Oh my God Laura, it's so loud!"

The girls crept to the railing that ran along the upstairs hall. Leaning over the banister, their hearts pounded in terror at the pandemonium below.

At that instant, the rocking chair that stood by the stove went sailing through the air past the stairs and parlor, crashing against the front door.

They screamed and grabbed each other again.

Laura, her eyes wild with fear, sobbed.

"What…what can be down there Becky?"

Another moan pulsed through the house. They heard the sound of china and glass crashing against the wall.

"Now it's in the pantry. Oh no Becky, Mother's dishes! It's smashing Mother's dishes. What do we do Becky? Oh my god, what do we do?"

Becky, her body shaking uncontrollably, heard herself scream as more furniture crashed against the front door so close to them.

The rhubarb preserves, that the girls put down that day, rolled down the hallway, the bottles smashing together against the door.

Laura, clutching Becky, shouted above the noise.

"Listen, it sounds like an animal in pain."

Above the crashing of furniture and crockery, a sobbing wail seemed to fill every corner of the house.

They stood rooted in complete terror.

"Quick Laura, get to your room! We've got to lock ourselves in."

Laura stood with her hands over her ears trying to block out the horrendous screeching and moaning coming from below.

They ran into Laura's room. Slamming and locking the door, they fell against it. The undeniable horror of their situation encompassed them.

Then total, complete, silence.

Laura grabbed Becky, sobbing in relief.

"Listen, it's stopped! The noise has stopped."

Becky, panting deeply, nodded; her hand pushing against her chest, trying to still the rapid pounding of her heart.

Trembling, they stood holding their breath. Listening for what seemed an eternity to the deathly silence below. Becky pushed Laura away and slowly eased the door open, straining to hear above the beating of her heart.

"Oh God Becky, please don't open the door.

Laura squealed with fear.

Becky tried to push the hysterical girl away.

"It's okay Laura."

She whispered.

"I think it's gone."

She slowly opened the door just far enough to stick her head out. Her breath still coming in short gasps, she turned to Laura who stood behind her wringing her hands.

She took a deep breath as tears of relief streamed down her face.

"Oh God Laura, I think it's finally gone."

She wiped her face with the back of her hand.

She shook a stunned Laura.

"It's okay Laura, it's gone."

Wailing moans sliced through their senses, curdling Becky's blood.

"Oh dear God Laura! Oh dear God!"

Becky slammed the door shut.

"What Becky? What?"

Becky ran for the armchair and started to drag it over to the door.

"Help me Laura! Help me, sobbed Becky. It's comin'! It's comin' for us!"

They could hear a heavy dragging sound coming towards them from the hall. The hair-raising din of moaning and wailing filled their very souls with horror.

Then came a thud that shook the upstairs, followed by another.

"Becky, Becky."

Laura screeched.

"It's coming up the steps. Oh my God it's going to kill us!"

Becky grabbed the wrought iron headboard of the bed and started dragging it across the floor.

"Help me Laura. Help me with the bed!"

They pulled and shoved until it leaned across the doorway. Using their last bit of strength, they lifted the heavy chair onto the bed, ramming it hard against the thick door.

The noise was deafening.

Becky sobbed.

"It's at the top of the steps Laura. Oh my God, it's almost here."

The wailing grew louder as the door started to buckle from the pounding. The weight of the bed wasn't able to keep the thing's strength at bay.

Screaming, Laura and Becky huddled together on the floor in the farthest corner of the room.

"We're going to die Becky."

Laura sobbed, her back pushed tightly against the wall.

Becky shouted above the wailing and pounding.

"Pray Laura. Pray as loud as you can."

Becky hollered.

"Our Father who...who art in heaven."

Laura screamed as another piece of the door let go.

"Pray with me, Laura!"

"Hallowed be thy name."

The banging and the wailing grew louder. A stench of a rotting animal permeated the room. Laura placed her hands over her face screaming as she tried to push herself even further against the wall, as the door split down the middle.

The stench was almost suffocating.

Becky pulled the hysterical girl from the corner.

"Get behind me Laura."

She grabbed the quilt from the floor and rolled it into a ball. With her other hand, she picked up a brass candlestick by Laura's bed and smashed at the glass in the window. She took the screaming Laura and wrapped her in the quilt and pushed her out. Still screaming, Laura fell on the roof of the back porch.

Becky shouted above the moaning.

"Jump Laura, jump to the ground!"

The bed went smashing against the back wall as Becky escaped through the window. The stench still so cloying that it seemed to ooze into every pore of her quivering body. She took a deep breath and jumped from the porch roof almost landing on top of Laura who lay prostrate on the moist grass.

As they retreated from the things clutches, it roared and wailed in total frustration. Sounds of complete destruction tore into the silence of the night. Moaning and wailing reached a credenza as a wing back chair flew through the opening of the window, missing them by inches and smashing into the well box.

"Run as fast as you can Laura. Run!"

Becky pulled a stunned Laura to her feet. Supporting each other they ran toward the safety of the farm.

Sobbing in terror, with the full moon leading them along the lonely dirt road, they ran from the evil that reigned in the house on the hill.

Finally they reached the sanctuary of the farmhouse. Becky left Laura exhausted on the bottom step. She pounded on the door until her legs buckled and she fell into her brother's arms.

"Becky? What in the name of...oh my God, Laura!"

Becky hung on to Bert, sobbing.

"I want Ma, Bert. Get Ma!"

Hours later, they sat around the kitchen table all except for Nana who rocked on her chair by the stove. Laura and Becky had composed themselves enough to tell their tale of horror. It was hard to believe, with the early morning sun streaming through the open window, the scope of horror that ensnared them just hours before.

Gus, who had arrived earlier, held Becky's hand as she described in detail the terror they had endured the previous evening.

He shook his head.

"It's hard to believe. I just can't take it all in."

Nana stopped rocking, both hands cupping a saucer of tea. With her eyes tightly shut, she tried to block out the horror that Becky and Laura had to endure.

"I can tell you one thing. This answers a lot of questions why people never stayed there long. Merciful Lord, this must have been going on for years."

An exhausted Laura leaned against Bert. She looked imploringly around the table.

"What do we tell people about last night?"

Elsie poured more tea from a large earthenware teapot, while barley bread and cheese lay untouched on the plates in front of them.

"I can't tell you what to do, but if it was left up to me I'd say nothin' to nobody. Fix up the mess and keep it to yourself. Somehow you're gonna have to get to the bottom of it, one way or the other."

Nana, rocking in her chair, leaned toward the table, her lips pressed so tightly together that only a narrow pink line emerged.

"I hate to break this to you child, on top of all the other burdens you're carryin', but I'm sure what you saw last night had somethin' to do with your pa's death."

A grief-stricken silence settled over the room, broken only by Laura's muffled sobbing as she pressed her face into Bert's shoulder.

Elsie eased her tired body down to an empty chair at the head of the table and clasped her hands tightly against her chest.

"Bert, go get the Reverend Owen, he's our only hope. Bring him to the house. Tell him we need to talk to him bad. We need help from the Lord. This is out of our hands."

Two hours later, Reverend Owen listened with unbridled horror as Laura and Becky related the events from the night before.

He sat at the table, his head continuously shaking in disbelief. Kind gray eyes widened with revulsion as the girls finished their tale.

"Are you absolutely sure that it wasn't a bear?"

Both Laura and Becky nodded their heads.

Becky swallowed, wiping the tears with the tips of her fingers when they threatened to flow again.

"That was no animal, Reverend. If you would have heard how angry it was when Laura and me escaped from the window. The chair that came crashing out of the window missed us by inches."

An hour after their meeting, Bert's wagon pulled up in front of Laura's house. Reverend Owen followed it close behind on his horse. With Gus's help, Elsie, Becky and Laura jumped down from the back of the wagon.

They stood outside the picket fence, silently staring at the house, waiting for the Reverend to dismount.

Bert turned to Laura.

"Is it locked?"

She shook her head.

"No, I usually don't lock the doors. I always felt so safe here."

Her lips trembled as her chin dropped to her chest in defeat.

"At least I use to. I guess I'll never be able to say that again."

Becky squeezed her friend's arm.

"We'll get through this Laura. Someday this will just seem like a bad dream."

Bert tried to open the door, but it would only give a few inches.

"Gus, give me a hand. There seems to be somethin' in the way."

Both men leaned with their shoulders against the door pushing as hard as they could. It gave a little bit more, but the opening still wasn't large enough to enter through.

Bert shook his head at Gus as they both stepped back from the door.

"Seems to be somethin' big blockin' the way."

Gus nodded.

"Okay Bert, let's give it all we got."

Both men braced their legs on the stoop and leaned all their weight into the door, pushing with both hands. With the sound of scrapping on the wide boards in the hall, the door finally opened far enough so that they could enter single file.

Reverend Owen took a small blue prayer book from a pocket in his frock and began praying. "Dear Father in heaven, keep us safe..."

Bert and Gus stood back and let the Reverend pass before following close behind him. Elsie, Laura and Becky were the last to enter the hall, or what was left of it.

They stood huddled inside the front door. Their minds unable to accept the total destruction that lay strewn before them.

The heavy pine wood of the kitchen table lay in jagged pieces against the wall closest to the door. A Boston rocker with the back ripped in half, as if it were made of paper, rocked wobbly on the pile of splintered wood.

Bert kicked what was left of the table standing in their way.

"Looks like this is what was keepin' us from openin' the door."

Reverend Owen crushed his prayer book to his heart, his bloodless lips moving in a silent prayer.

Becky shook Gus's arm and pointed, fear constricting her face.

"Oh dear Lord Gus, look at the steps."

Every rung of wood in the banister had been pulled up from the edge of the stairs. It was as if they had been harvested by the demon and then stacked there to dry.

The walls on either side of the hall had ugly dragging gouges, almost running parallel with each other, so deep that Reverend Owen could place his hand inside them.

Bunched close together, they kept touching each other for comfort and support as they moved to the back of the house.

They entered the kitchen.

Laura started to cry. It was completely demolished.

Becky pulled at her mother's arm.

"Oh Ma, look at the pump."

The hardwood handle was splintered into a thousand tiny pieces and dangled from the metal spout. The curved opening bent and twisted toward the ceiling.

Bert took his mother by the arm.

"Ma, I want you to take the girls out the back door while we stay here."

Fear filled Elsie's face.

"Why? What are you gonna do Bert?"

He stared out to the mangled stairs in the front hall, locking eyes with Gus and the Reverend, who nodded their heads in unison.

"We have to go up there and we don't want you near the house when we do it."

Laura wrung her hands.

"No Bert", she pleaded, "What if it's still there?"

"Laura we're going to be okay. But to be on the safe side, I want you womenfolk out of harm's way."

Reverend Owen looked around.

"He's right Elsie, outside is the best place for you to be now."

Gus led the way to the back porch. They stepped gingerly over pieces of wood that had been thrown in every direction. The screen door ripped from its hinges, leaned against what was left of the mangled wood box by the back stairs.

Becky picked up the curtains that had been torn from the broken window. Bits of glass fell to her feet. She bit her lip, as Laura pulled her father's coat out of the woodpile, torn and ripped almost beyond recognition.

"I helped father pick this out just before we moved here. Now look at it, worthless, just like everything else."

She shut her eyes tightly, trying hard to curb the tears that threatened to overwhelm her.

The curtains fell from Becky's numb fingers, as she pulled her shawl closer to her shivering body.

"Oh my God."

She moaned.

"You can still feel its cold hatred."

Reverend Owen shook his head in bewilderment.

"What in heaven's name was it?"

He looked around, emotionally exhausted.

Laura stared at him helplessly.

"Did this happen because of me?"

The reverend shook his head.

"It can't be anything to do with you, child. You've only lived here for such a short time. How can it be possible that it could cause this much havoc?"

Laura grimaced.

"Look around Reverend. This is the aftermath of its destruction."

She stared despondently at the pathetic pile of rags that had been her father's coat.

"We were in the raging heart of it."

Gus and Bert cleared the final pieces of wood and debris from the back doorway.

Elsie grabbed Bert and wrapped her arms around him.

"You listen to me son, the first thing you hear that ain't right you leave this house as fast as those long legs will carry you."

She glared at the other men, tears blinding her eyes. "And that goes for all of you."

They nodded, standing their ground until the women were safely out of the house.

Elsie reluctantly led the way into the warmth of the late morning sunshine, with Laura and Becky close behind her. As they stood under Laura's bedroom window, they could hear Reverend Owen shouting the Lord's Prayer as he slowly climbed the battered steps.

The prayers stopped. Minutes seemed like hours to the women who waited anxiously below, until they saw Bert's grim face lean through the gaping hole.

"There's nothing here."

Becky wet her dry lips.

"Is it safe to come up?"

Gus, his face pale, stood by Bert.

"It don't pay for you to come up now, it will just upset you more. I think you've had all you can handle for a spell."

Bert nodded in agreement.

"Gus is right. You wait there 'til we come down. It don't pay for you to come back in here."

Becky sighed, relieved that the men had made the decision for them. Just this once, she agreed with her brother.

While they waited for the men to join them, Becky walked to the well and picked up the broken pieces of the chair. One of the wooden legs was embedded firmly in the planked platform of the well box. She pulled on the leg, dislodging part of the platform.

She stopped and stared astonished at what lay below the broken board.

"Ma, Laura, come here, I found somethin."

She removed a dirty bundle of cloth that appeared to be rotted leather from between the rocks piled by the well.

Elsie and Laura knelt in the cool grass beside her.

Her mother leaned over her shoulder.

"What is it Becky?"

They watched as she unrolled the bundle until a small tin box rolled into her outstretched hand. Red flakes of rust floated to the ground as Becky gingerly handled it.

Laura, her eyes wide, stared at Becky's hand.

"What do you think it is?"

Just then the men came into the healing sunshine.

Laura ran to Bert.

"Oh Bert, I'm so glad you're okay."

Reverend Owen shook his head in amazement.

"Now that I've seen the destruction in the house, it's a miracle you survived all that."

Becky nodded her head.

"I'll never forget that stench to my dyin' day."

Bert put his hand around her waist and pulled her close to his side.

"I know what you mean. Sometime we would catch a whiff of somethin' bad. It must of been somethin' horrible, being right there in the middle of it."

He noticed the rusty box in Laura's hand.

"What have you got there girl?"

"It's a tin box. I found it when I pulled the chair leg out of the side of the well. I tried to get it open, but its rusted shut. Gus, do you have your jackknife on you?"

Gus nodded and opened his knife and passed it to Becky. She wedged the tip of the blade into the underside of the lid.

"I think I almost got it."

She pushed hard and the lid flipped open. The box turned upside down and a small dirty bundle of cloth fell to the grass by her feet.

Bert picked it up, catching a small book as it unraveled from a cloth.

Reverend Owen joined them by the well.

"What is it Bert?"

He gingerly opened the cover.

"I don't know, it looks like a journal of some kind."

They all stood around him craning their necks to get a peek.

Bert turned a mildewed page.

"It looks like it's written in German."

"May I see?"

Reverend Owen took the book and sat down on the other side of the well box.

"Yes it is, let me see if I can translate it."

He started to translate.

"This is the diary of Obediah Hynnick."

He shook his head.

"This is going to be difficult. Some of the pages have stuck together and the writing is so small in places it's unreadable."

Elsie pushed herself up from the grass, shaking her skirt.

"I don't know about you, but I've had enough of this place for a while. Why don't we go home, clean up and I'll make us somethin' to eat. You'll stay Reverend and partake with us? And then maybe you can cipher this book."

After they had eaten, Elsie found an old cloth and laid it on the kitchen table in front of Reverend

Owen. He took the book from his pocket and placed it on the cloth. Anxiously, they waited as he tried to translate it.

"I think it reads, 'Only I know, what sins the fruits of my loin have done'. And then it says, ''The Lord's wrath will swoop down and punish'."

He paused, squinting at the book.

"The next part is very difficult to make out, but I think it says 'I am the right hand of the Lord. Let His will be done. For no Jezebel shall live to bear the fruits of her fornication'."

Elsie placed a mug of tea in front of him.

"What does he mean Reverend?"

Nana, who rocked in her chair, spoke up for the first time.

"Sounds to me like some poor girl was with child."

"Nana, didn't you say that your pa told you that Obediah Hynnick had a daughter?"

She thought for a moment, nodding her head.

'Yes, he did. He tried to go a courting only to be told that his daughter and his wife had gone to nurse a relative."

Becky jumped up and grabbed a slate and chalk from the shelf next to the stove.

"Tell me again what the first sentence says."

Reverend Owen turned back to the first page of the diary.

"I hope I'm translating this right. 'I and the Lord know what sins the fruits of my loins have done'."

Becky wrote, 'fruits of my loins'.

She looked up at the reverend.

"And the next one."

"Well it says, 'The Lord's wrath will swoop down from the heavens and punish' and the last sentence is, 'No Jezebel shall live to bear the fruits of her fornication'."

Becky wrote the last line down and read it silently. She gasped and looked around the table, the blood draining from her face.

"Oh my merciful heavens!"

Gus jumped up and kneeled by her chair.

"What's wrong Becky?"

Becky looked around the table.

"Don't you understand what the reverend is readin'?"

She put her chalk down and looked across the table at Reverend Owen.

"Do you know what you just read?"

Puzzled, he shook his head, staring at the book.

"I don't know what you mean Becky. It sounds like he was very troubled."

Becky shook her head.

"No, listen to what you translated, 'fruits of my loins' "

"Then you said, 'swoop down and punish'."

She looked around the table.

"Don't any of you understand what was goin' on?"

Elsie put her hand to her mouth.

"Oh no, you don't mean…"

She caught the look of confirmation in her daughter's eyes.

Becky nodded her head.

"That's right Ma, listen to the last line, 'For no Jezebel shall live to bear the fruits of her fornication'. Nana was right, this girl was going to have a baby."

"Dear God child, what are you sayin?"

Becky took a deep breath.

"I'm sayin' Ma that Obedeiah Hynnick found out that his daughter was in the family way and he killed her. Then he told people that she went away and then…"

Laura interrupted.

"But, what about the mother?"

Becky looked at the minister.

"Can you translate any of the other writin'?"

He turned the yellowed pages.

"I'll try, this is in such poor condition."

He turned another page.

"There's more writing. Something' about 'protecting her sinful seed,' and then, 'shall perish in the fires of damnation', or the last word might be...hell."

He looked up apologizing.

"I'm sorry this is very hard to read. I have a magnifying glass back in my study."

Becky wrote down the last words that he had translated and then read them out loud.

"Protecting her sinful seed shall perish."

Becky put her chalk down on the slate and looked at their troubled faces.

"There can only be one answer. I think he killed them both and he's still hauntin' Laura's house."

Laura whispered.

"My house is haunted?" What am I going to do?"

Bert, shrugging his shoulders, covered her hand and squeezed it.

"I don't know girl."

He looked at Reverend Owen.

"Can you tell us what to do?"

Reverend Owen sat at the table, his hands clasped in front of his bewildered face, shaking his head.

"No, I can't. In all my years, I've never encountered this before."

He looked at Laura.

"Have faith my child, we'll get to the bottom of this."

He pulled a gold watch out of his vest pocket and flipped open the cover.

"I'm afraid I have to leave. I'm already late for a meeting with the Senior Warden of the parish."

Rising from the table, his glance took in everyone.

"I think that it would be best for all, if this never left the room."

He looked at Laura.

"Maybe if I take the book home and look at it with my glass, I might be able to decipher it better."

Laura nodded and Elsie rose from the table passing the book to him.

"When will you be ridin' through again?"

"Tomorrow afternoon. That will give me time to look at this book."

"Then come and take supper with us."

"Thank-you, Elsie. I try never to pass up one of your meals."

He looked at Laura.

"Try not to worry, we'll see this through."

Opening the screen door, he turned and faced them.

"I cannot stress this enough. We must not repeat a word about this to anyone."

Gus shook his head.

"Don't worry Reverend, who would believe us if we did."

He waved.

"Until tomorrow, God bless you."

They watched through the kitchen window as he mounted his horse and rode towards Lunenburg.

The next day seemed to drag on forever. The men worked extra hard catching up on neglected chores, while the women were busy in the kitchen.

Reclining on the cot by the stove, Laura watched Elsie kneading bread dough.

"Please let me help with something. I feel worthless just lying here."

Elsie stopped kneading, taking in Laura's face.

"You're still weak from your fall and if you rest there and behave yourself for a little longer you can peel some vegetables for supper. If not, I'll make you go to your bed."

Laura smiled at Elsie's good-natured scolding.

"Yes Ma."

Becky entered the kitchen carrying a basket of clothes.

"It's no good arguin' with Ma, cause it don't pay."

She stopped and took a deep breath.

"Oh my Ma, the kitchen smells so good. It's makin' my mouth water."

Elsie nodded, flour floating in the air around her as she patted the dough into two balls.

"The Reverend likes his food and I want to give him a good meal."

At the word reverend, Laura sat up.

"I just hope he has some good news."

"Don't worry child, he'll know what to do."

As Elsie turned away and reached for the bread pans, the look on her face did not mirror her words.

When the supper dishes were cleared and washed, they sat around the table and waited for Reverend Owen to speak.

He sighed and looked at Laura.

"I'm afraid, my dear, that Becky figured out what happened so many years ago at your house."

He pulled out a folded piece of paper.

"I wrote down everything I could translate. It wasn't easy, what with his religious ramblings and illegible handwriting, and I didn't dare consult with anyone else. This afternoon I had time to check the Lutheran Church records and I found out that the daughter's name was Hannah. She was about eighteen years old when she died by her father's hand."

Gus sighed deeply.

"So he did kill her?"

The Reverend nodded.

"I'm afraid so."

Bert cleared his throat.

"You got any ideas what we should do?"

Reverend Owen's eyes locked with Bert's.

"Yes I do, we have to go back and find the graves of Hannah and her mother and give them a proper Christian burial."

Elsie's head snapped up.

"Her mother?"

He nodded his head.

"I'm afraid so. He killed her as well."

Laura eyes, wide with horror, stared at him.

"And this will make the thing leave my house?"

He sat across from Laura folding the paper over in his hands.

"To be honest with you, I don't know, but it's a start."

"You can't go back! What if it attacks you?"

"It's the only way my dear."

"I may as well tell you what else I found out. Obediah is responsible for the death of Hannah's lover."

Elsie drew in a deep breath.

"Merciful heavens, the man was a monster."

He unfolded the paper again and looked around.

"This is what I gleaned from his diary. Hannah's lover wanted to take her away and marry her, but Obediah went into such a rage when he caught them running away together that he stabbed the man with his knife. After he stabbed him, he ran

95

after Hannah beating her with his bare hands. His wife tried to pull him away, only to be thrown to the floor and stabbed with the same knife. After his murdering frenzy, he dragged Hannah's unconscious body down to the cellar and buried her in the corner next to the foundation."

He stopped, folded the piece of paper up and put it back in his pocket, looking around the table.

"Later that night, he buried his wife under the lilac tree. The last words that he wrote in his diary was that Hannah was still alive when he buried her."

Bert wiped away the beads of perspiration that covered his upper lip.

"Oh my God, what a hellish way to go."

He stood up and motioned for Gus to follow.

"Let's get this over with. Let's go find those bodies."

Laura grabbed Bert's arm and tried to pull him down to his seat.

"Bert, please don't go. It will kill you just like it tried to kill us."

"It will be okay Laura, seems to me that thing only comes out at night."

Reverend Owen pulled out his pocket watch checking the time with the clock on the mantle.

"It's quarter past the five now, I suggest that we gather some tools and take them to Laura's house.

The least we can do is to give those poor souls a proper burial."

The women, filled with dreadful misgivings, stood clinging to each other on the verandah watching as the wagon rattled out of sight.

It was a shallow grave. The roots of the old lilac tree had shifted some of the bones. Almost reverently, they removed the mother's remains from her resting place and placed them on a blanket. When all of the bones had been collected, Reverend Owen laid them gently in the wooden tool chest that they had brought with them.

The sun was starting to set as they approached the back of the house. They stood in front of the cellar entrance where large flat doors covered the opening. Gus hesitated and pulled the heavy doors back, hooking them to the side of the house. Lighting the lanterns, he braced himself before stepping down into Hannah's dank, dark tomb. They followed him, Reverend Owen clutching the shovels and an extra lantern, while Bert followed behind carrying the makeshift coffin.

Reverend Owen raised his lantern looking around the low-beamed chamber.

He placed it on the dirt floor.

"Now, according to his diary, Hannah's grave should be about here."

He held his lantern as high as he could and pointed to the dim corner where green slime oozed to the ground over granite stones. Bert and Gus, grabbing the shovels from the ground, bent their backs to the grisly chore in front of them. The only noise was the sound of the shovels hitting the hard packed earth.

Bert raised his shovel. A tattered, filthy rag clung to the metal. His voice was devoid of emotion from the senseless tragedy of bygone years.

"I think we found her Reverend."

Tiny pebbles rolling down the uneven steps of the cellar completely paralyzed the three men.

The Reverend sucked in his breath, both hands covering his heart.

"Oh my soul and heaven!"

He gasped.

"I don't think this is very wise my dears."

Becky and Laura held their lanterns as high as the entrance would allow them. Faltering on the uneven steps, they walked towards the men.

Bert threw his shovel down. His harsh voice filled with emotion, as he glared at the girls.

"I thought we told you to stay out of this. You march right around and get for home."

Gus nodded his head, as both hands clenched the handle of the shovel.

"That goes for you too, Becky. You listen to your brother. This is no place for you women-folk."

"I'm sorry Bert, but we just can't stay home. The waiting was horrible. We had to come."

"Ma let you come, Becky?"

"We snuck out when she went to the chicken coop."

Laura stared at the wooden chest.

"Did you find them Bert?"

"We did, we found the mother or what was left of her."

Gus nodded, his voice shaking with emotion.

"And we just found the daughter."

Bert pointed to the steps with his shovel.

"Now get out of here and go home."

Without warning, both of the heavy flat cellar doors slammed shut, separating them from the outside world. Laura and Becky both screamed in unison. The feeble flames from their lanterns wavering before being extinguished by some unknown hand. Stunned, the men stood in deep shadows as the pungency of the open dank grave heightened their fear.

Reverend Owen rallied first, trying to reassure everybody.

"Now girls that was a...a shock, but I'm sure that the wind just blew them shut."

Gus's next words tore the contrived smile from Reverend Owen's lips.

"No it didn't Reverend, I hooked both doors to the house before we entered."

Laura screamed.

"Oh my God! It's back! It's in the corner!"

There in the farthest corner of the cellar, two orange lights started to glow with a sickly haze. Thick foggy smoke materialized from out of nowhere, slowly swirling and moving around the orange spheres forming a head.

They watched in complete horror, as the unholy vapor thickened and meshed into the outline of something almost human. The smell of decay encompassed them.

Reverend Owen, his legs buckling, clutched the post in front of him. Bert and Gus grabbed the girls, pushing them against the wall. They stood braced, acting as human shields. Becky could feel the cold wet rocks from the foundation dig deep into her back.

Laura clung to her whimpering, as they were pushed even further back against the foundation.

Gus whispered, his voice cracking with disbelief.

"Merciful God! What is it?"

Both women screeched as the satanic shadow took a faltering step towards them and then another. With each jerky movement it made, the ground vibrated beneath their feet.

This thing from hell could taste their fear, feeding, growing more powerful and louder as it loomed closer. The moaning forming undeniable words to Bert; causing the hairs on his body to stand ridged with fear.

"KILL...KILL...KILL."

"Do somethin' Reverend! My God man, do somethin'!"

Coughing and gagging, they pressed their hands over their faces as the stench of rotting flesh became almost unbearable. Reverend Owen reached into his pocket searching for his bible. His hands trembling with terror, as evil inched toward him.

With both hands, he held his bible high in front of his body, a crusader fighting his demonic nemesis, shouting above the moaning and wailing.

"In the name of the Father, Son and Holy Ghost. Be gone! Be gone I tell you! Be gone!"

Collecting every ounce of his faith, he stepped toward it demanding obedience. It recoiled for a moment and then lashed out, sucking him up only to toss him to the ground. They could feel its foul breath, surrounding them and knew that their end was near. Bert grabbed Laura and held her tightly in his arms. Gus, with tears streaming down his face, wrapped his arms around Becky.

His lips close to her ear, he whispered.

"I love you Becky girl and don't you ever forget it."

They watched in horror as Reverend Owen crawled toward the beast from hell. His bible still clutched in his hand, still demanding it to leave.

Suddenly, feathery gray mists gathered and swirled forming a column directly in front of them. The soft scent of bygone lilacs overshadowed the putrid smell of decay. The column fanned out toward it, a silhouette of a woman emerging in front of their astonished eyes.

Laura sobbed.

"Oh my God! It's her, it's the mother. She's tryin' to protect us."

The black fiend recoiled and roared with frustration as she pushed it further away from them. Two old foes battling for complete supremacy.

Reverend Owen pulled himself up shouting above the deafening noise.

"In the name of the Father, the Son and the Holy Ghost, be gone! Go back to the depths of hell where you belong."

It roared and bellowed in defeat, as the orange light flickered Disappearing in front of their very eyes and with its departure... silence.

The woman, for they could tell it had been a woman, turned and faced them. The cellar was infused with a soft pale light. She seemed to falter unsure of what to do next.

With the bible outstretched in his hand, still gasping for breath, Reverend Owen stumbled toward her, making the sign of the cross in front of him, gently repeating,

"In the name of the Father, the Son and the Holy Ghost, rest in peace."

As he uttered these words, the room filled with the cloying scent of dead lilacs. Flickering for a moment, the light died, leaving them again in total darkness.

Bert stumbled to the entrance, flung the doors back and they ran up into the welcoming coolness of the sweet night air.

The next evening at dusk with the crickets chirping in the pasture above the farm, they said a final prayer over the flower covered grave of Hannah and her mother. They left as they came, quietly giving thanks to a woman they had never known.

As the sun set in the west, warm pink rays shimmered against the humble slate marker, illuminating the carved inscription that read...

SHE ROSE AND CONQUERED

TO SLEEP FOREVER

THE FIRE, LOW on the grate, snapped and hissed from the rain dripping down the chimney, as the stranger finished his story. The innkeeper rose and stretched, throwing a large junk of wood on the low flames. He gathered empty tankards from the table in front of his guests. Some he refilled, while others he left at the bar. The stranger sat facing the passengers, as if he were a schoolmaster reading to storm stranded students.

Their eyes were riveted to his large calloused hands motionless on the book. They sighed with relief as he turned another page and began to read.

The Weeping Walls

R. R. Durling pulled back hard on the reins, causing the pair of Belgians to halt in the middle of the circular driveway. Hanging on to the back of the seat, he stepped down to the ground and gazed in awe at the breathtaking scene below.

"Just look at that view Jake, did you ever see such beauty?"

Jake Sarty smiled.

"I can't say I have Uncle. Not for a long time."

Below them, the LaHave River meandered along its banks. The quiet waters mirroring the spectacular colors of autumn's brilliant foliage. Ancient trees with their majestic branches bowing to the water's edge, paid homage to the river flowing before them. Screeching, an eagle circled overhead. Swooping down, it skimmed across transparent waters, catching its first salmon of the day.

Jake filled his lungs with the sweet September air.

"I'd say Uncle, that this is pretty close to heaven."

They opened the back glass door of the carriage hearse, dragging the first coffin toward them.

After laying it down, Durling stopped and looked once more at the panoramic vision.

"No matter how close to heaven you think you are in this life Jake,"

He paused, reaching for the brass handle of the second coffin.

"Hell is never far away."

Jake, his face grim, watched the black crepe on the mourning wreath flutter, as the door of the Italian style home opened. On the curved brick entrance, a young woman attired in black stood waiting between the wide white pillars.

She was the prettiest little thing he ever saw. Hair as black as ravens' wings, too wild to be tamed, curled out in every direction from under the lace scrap tilted on her head. From her creamy flawless face, large green eyes, wet with unshed tears, watched as he walked toward her.

"Mornin' Miss, I'm Jake Sarty."

One lonely tear fell from the corner of her eye.

"I'm tinkin' you're the undertaker then?" The soft lilt of her Irish drawl seemed like music to his ears.

Jake nodded, stunned by her beauty. His fingers tugged at the collar tightening around his throat.

"Yes we are."

"Then I'll be a waitin' here to show you where to go."

Jake rejoined his uncle at the back of the hearse. Bending together, they picked the first empty coffin up from the grass. A smile eased over the older man's lips, his eyes twinkling at his nephew.

"You know Jake, when you're talkin' to pretty girls its best if you don't keep your mouth tore open."

The older man groaned as he shifted the weight of the coffin in his hands.

"Unless you're tryin' to impress her by catchin' flies."

Later, in the elegant front room, burnished teak coffins of the two young sisters laid on extended mahogany tables. The tables, draped in black crepe, stood against a side wall covered in luxurious silk. Blanketing the coffins, enormous sprays of soft pink roses cascaded to the floor as tightly closed buds caressed the burgundy broadloom.

Jake stood discreetly inside the double French doors that separated the spacious front room from the large airy foyer, observing friends of the family paying their last respects.

His heart was touched as he watched Edward Oickle wrap his arm around his wife's waist as they stood by the side of the coffins. His other arm pulled his five year old son, Neddy, close to his side, as they spoke to their friends and neighbors.

Intent on the scene before him, Jake jumped when the Irish beauty touched him on the arm.

He whispered.

"You scared a year from my life girl."

She gently touched his arm again.

"You were chasin' dreams so you den hear me the first time. I was a sayin', would you be sayin' no to a cup of tea right now?"

Jake, suddenly tongue-tied, groped for words. He could only nod his head.

"Then follow me and I'll be showin' you where to go."

"I'll wait 'til Uncle can come, he's outside feedin' the horses."

She smiled up at him, her green eyes sparkling.

"The kitchen is at the end of the hall and down the steps. Your tea will be waitin' for you."

Jake turned his head as his uncle entered the front door. "Here's Uncle now."

"Then I'll be showin' you both the way."

They followed close behind, blue carpet thick beneath their feet. The faint rustling of her skirt against the carpet infringed upon the silence that surrounded them.

Mouth-watering smells greeted them as they entered the welcoming kitchen. The table, its center filled with plates of large round sweet rolls, stood in a double bay window overlooking a kitchen garden.

A plump middle age woman greeted them, as she stood stirring a large steaming pot. Fine wisps of hair, in various shades of gray, lay limp against her flushed cheeks.

"Good day Ruben. It's been a long time. Come in and sit a spell."

She smiled at Jake as he followed behind his uncle.

"And who's this young man with you?"

"This Effie, is my sister's boy, Jake."

"Nice to meet ya Jake. And you've already met Abby here. Girl, put some food in front of these men. I'm sure they can use it."

She watched them as they sat down in the Bass River chairs at the end of the table.

"Pour the men some tea and then pour some for ourselves. You must be run right off your feet girl what with everything that's going on upstairs."

Abby poured the tea and sat down sighing, as she pulled the steaming mug toward her.

"That I am, Mrs. Hull."

Mrs. Hull stirred the large pot one last time and pushed it to the back of the stove. The mouth-watering aroma of simmering applesauce filled the kitchen.

"There, now I'm ready for my tea too."

Easing her tired body into the chair next to Jake, she sighed pulling a soft white cloth from her apron pocket. Wiping the moisture from her flushed face, she leaned back against the chair and closed her eyes.

"It's been quite a day, hasn't it Abby?"

"Indeed it has and I hope to say that I'm not lookin' for another, for a long time."

She reached for the plate and took one of the sweet buns before passing it to Jake, her eyes full of concern.

"It's not the dyin' that I'm talkin' about. My da always said, you live you die and that's how it is. It's this other ting I don't know what to do bout."

Mrs. Hull put her mug down hard, her usual pleasant voice chastising.

"Abby MacDonald, I don't think it's wise to talk about that now. Not with folks outside the family."

Abby stared at Durling, her Irish eyes full of questions.

"You being the undertaker, now I'm tinkin' people have told you some fearful tings."

Durling, raising his eyebrows in thought, pondered over his next words.

"You're right there girl, I've been told things that no one else has ever known because of what I do. They know that I'll be as quiet as the grave."

Mrs. Hull took a sip of her tea and swirled the leaves around in her cup. Her forehead creased in anxiety.

"Well, we need to tell someone."

This is hard to believe Ruben, but the day before those poor little lambs drowned in the river, the walls…the wall in their bedrooms started to weep."

Jake sat up in his chair, the fragrant roll all but forgotten on his plate.

"Weep? What do you mean weep?"

Mrs. Hull took a long drink of her tea.

"That's the only words that can describe what we saw."

She reached for the sugar bowl and dropped three heaping teaspoons of sugar in her tea, stirring it before she continued.

"Abby here was the one that spotted it first."

Abby nodded, her eyes round as she spoke.

"As sure as we're sittin' here, I went to the room to clean and there on the wall were two wet spots in the shape of eyes. As I got nearer to the wall my heart almost stopped beatin' for what I saw."

She stopped talking, lowered her eyes and became very intent on the tiny pink flowers on her mug.

Jake waited for her to continue, but she sat there quietly.

Everyone around the table had their eyes locked on her. Jake took another mouthful of the hot tea.

"Well, what did you see?"

Abby looked at the cook, who nodded her head encouragingly.

She pressed her lips together before pearly white teeth chewed on her lower lip, agonizing over the rest of her story. She crossed herself twice before clenching her mug tightly in both hands.

"I couldn't believe what I was seeing. I moved as close as I could. Tiny tears ran down the wall and plopped to the floor... disappearin' as soon as they hit the carpet."

Jake stared at her trying to comprehend what she was saying, but her words wouldn't register.

"How can that be? That ain't possible."

Abby's eyes snapped at him in annoyance.

"Are you doubtin' me now? As sure as I'm sittin' here, tears ran down the walls and disappeared. The floor where they dropped was as dry as all the bones in St. Michael's Cathedral."

Jake could hardly believe what Abby was saying. His feelings were mirrored on his uncle's face.

"There must be some mistake. It has to be a leak in the house somewhere."

Abby rolled her eyes, her mouth grim.

"A leak is it? You'll not be sayin' that when you hear the rest of it. Dere's more to it."

She took a deep breath, glanced at Mrs. Hull, who nodded.

"Go on girl, don't stop now."

"When we walked through the door of the rooms, we could hear the sound of soft cryin' comin' from the walls."

Jake swallowed, hoping that the lump that had lodged at the base of his throat would disappear.

"Cryin'? Oh that can't be."

Abby nodded her head daring him with her snapping green eyes to call her a liar.

"It was as if you were in a church full of mourners cryin' softly. It seemed to come from every corner of the room, but just as soon as you crossed back into the hall, the cryin' stopped. It was the scariest sound I ever heard. Every hair on my body rose up."

Jake licked his dry lips. He took a long drink from his mug.

"It had to be a wind whistlin' around the windows, that can sound almost human at times."

Abby shook her head, her voice determined.

"It was no wind that was doin' that sobbin', was it Mrs. Hull?"

"No dear, I'm afraid that it wasn't. You may as well tell them the rest of it."

Abby watched them sitting together at the end of the table, their eyes wide with disbelief.

"It wasn't water that dropped to the floor in that room."

She glanced at Mrs. Hull, who nodded her support.

"It was blood."

"Blood?" Jake just sat and stared at both women.

"You mean blood dripped from the walls?"

Ruben was almost speechless.

"Now girl, are you sure it was blood?"

Mrs. Hull nodded her head.

"Oh it was blood alright. I touched it."

Jake couldn't believe what he was hearing.

"What?"

Abby's dark green eyes mirroring the horror she had seen, crossed herself.

"Saints preserve us, she did! I fell to the floor and called on every saint I could think of to protect her when she let them drops touch her hands."

Mrs. Hull put her hand on Abby's arm.

"It's okay dear, I'll take it from here."

She watched the two men sitting at her table, their jaws slack with horror. Her body shuddered with the memory.

"I know blood when I see it, and that was blood."

She stared at the men, weighing her next words.

"Warm blood."

A cloud drifted across the sun sucking the cheerful light from the kitchen, leaving it in shadows.

Jake cleared his throat, his voice shaken.

"Is it...is it still there?"

Mrs. Hull shook her head.

"No, it's gone now, nothin' remains. My heart shrank in fear as soon as I saw it for I knew that we were headed for a spell of grief. Then when we discovered that the girls were missin', I could hardly do my job. Later the same day, they found the little rowboat upside down in the river with their lifeless bodies tangled in among the dead tree roots by the riverbank. When they pulled them from the river and carried them back to the house, it all stopped. No more cryin'. The blood stopped flowin' without so much as leaving a stain behind."

Durling pushed his empty mug away, his eyes wide with disbelief.

"You mean it's gone? There's not a trace of it left? No stain, nothin'?"

She looked around the table, her voice just above a whisper.

"Have you ever heard anythin' like that before Ruben?"

He shook his head.

"I can't say that I have. That's a new one for the books, but you don't have to worry Effie about hearing this someplace else, cause Jake here and me won't be tellin' a living soul. Will we lad?"

Jake, his face pale, shook his head.

"No sir, we won't. Who'd believe us if we did."

A bell over the door of the kitchen rang urgently causing them to flinch in their chairs.

The undertaker pulled out his watch, checking the time. Standing up, he placed his hand on Effie's shoulder.

"It's safe with us Effie. It will go no further than this kitchen. I wouldn't still be in this business if I told everythin' I knew. So don't fret about it gettin' out."

He looked at his watch one last time before placing it back in the bottom pocket of his black woolen vest.

"Now Jake, I think upstairs is ready for us."

The funeral procession made its way into the maple-lined drive of Brookside Cemetery. Jake eased the horses around the ornate green fountain at the head of the lily pond. The smiling gargoyles spouting water seemed to mock them as they rode by. Ducks, their wings flapping in the still water, scurried to the far end of the pond as the huge horses clopped toward them.

Warm gentle breezes ruffed the trickling waters of the fountain, spraying the hot undertakers with a welcoming mist of cool water.

Jake stopped the animals in the lane between the lily pond and a grass-tiered hill. Two rounded mounds of dark moist earth lay like beacons beckoning the mourners to come closer. Reverend Duff, his prayer book in his hand, led the eight pallbearers as they carried the cumbersome coffins up the stone steps to the waiting graves.

The open black carriage of the family stopped behind the hearse. Jake could hear the sobs of Della Oickle as her husband helped her, their son and Abby from the carriage. Abby noticed Jake out of the corner of her eye and smiled sadly as she followed close behind the family.

Reverend Duff stepped up to the graves and waited. Edward, with Della clinging to his arm, followed the pallbearers up the three short stone steps to the first level of the hill and the waiting black cavities that would soon be her sisters' final resting place.

Jake and his uncle watched from the side of the hearse as the gravediggers slowly lowered the coffins into the ground.

Edward, now holding his wife tightly in his arms stared at the graves. Della's long face veil fluttered in the breeze showing glimpses of her grief stricken face, as her head rested on her husband's shoulder. Bewildered, Neddy clung to Abby's hand as Reverend Duff read the burial rites for the dead.

Two evenings later, in the carriage house on Phoenix Street, Ruben leaned against a pile of pine planks stacked in the corner of the workshop. The sweet smell of fresh wood shavings permeated the air. Sucking hard on his pipe, he lit the blackened bowl and inspected Jake's work through a smoky haze.

Jake attached the last brass handle on the coffin and turned to face his uncle.

"What do you think Uncle, one of my best ones yet?"

"It's a good one Jake, but remember that this is a six-footer and Mrs. Langille was only a little thing. Don't forget to put a partition up from the bottom so she won't slide around when the pallbearers pick the coffin up and carry it."

Nodding his head, Jake polished the brass handles.

"You know Uncle, the story we heard the other day at the Oickle house? That was a pretty hard story to take to heart."

Ruben sucked on his pipe and removed it from his mouth pointing the tip at Jake.

"You know Lad, I've been on this earth a lot longer than what you have and I can tell you right now that the story you heard the other day will not be the strangest you'll hear before you die."

Jake stared, his mouth dropping.

"You mean that you believe what they told us?"

Ruben puffed on his pipe, the smell of the wood chips mingling with the scent of tobacco. He puffed a few more times before nodding his head.

"Yep, I do. You know, I really wanted to know more about that wall but time escaped us there. Now, we'll never find out."

Jake pulled the coffin from the two sawhorses and grinned up at his uncle.

"Don't be too sure about that. Yesterday I asked Abby if she wanted to step out with me and we're goin' to the bandstand across the river Sunday afternoon."

Abby and Jake sat on the riverbank listening to the music drifting from the new bandstand. It was a lovely fall day, as the last dregs of summer's warmth fought for a foothold against the crisp fall air.

"The band sure does a good job playin', don't they Abby?"

Jake waited for her to answer him, but she stared silently down the river, not uttering a word.

"Abby, did you hear me girl?"

She turned to him puzzled.

"Did you say somethin' Jake?"

"I asked if you liked the music."

His voice was tinged with annoyance.

"Aren't you havin' a good time? I can take you home."

"Home? That's the last place I want to be. I love the music. It's just that I have a lot on my mind. I was tinkin' bout somethin' else."

"A blind man could figure that out. I spoke to you two times and you never answered. You just stared down the river."

"I'm so sorry Jake, but I'm so troubled."

"What's wrong Abby, you can tell me, I won't tell anyone, I promise. You have to share it with someone."

"The saints preserves us, you wouldn't believe me anyway."

As tears ran down her face, she looked at Jake with such sorrow that he felt remorse for his earlier words.

Abby hid her face from his view with her gloved hands and began crying with complete despair, leaving Jake absolutely bewildered.

"Abby girl? What on earth is wrong?"

Shaking her head, she cried even harder.

"I can't. I can't."

Finally the crying subsided and she gazed at him through tear-drenched lashes, but I've got to tell someone. It's hurtin' somethin' fierce tryin' to keep this inside me. I swore on my dear mother's grave that I wouldn't tell."

She grabbed Jake's hands with both of hers.

"Promise me you won't tell a single soul."

Jake could only nod his head.

"It's the walls. They've started again."

Jake stared at her. He could feel his mouth hanging open.

"What? Are you sure?"

"As sure as I'm sittin' here. Mrs. Hull and me, we don't know what to do."

"What room is it in?"

Abby started to cry again. The harsh sobbing turned into little whimpers.

"It's in little Neddy's room and we don't know what to do."

"Well, where is he now?"

"They've all gone to Boston on one of Mr. Oickle's ships. They're expected back late Thursday. I'm so afeared. Mrs. Hull can't take much more. She's taken to her bed with a fearful headache. It's worse than before. You can hear cryin' all over the house. It just won't stop. I'm so afeared that somethin' is gonna happen to little Neddy."

She started to cry again. Jake stood up and helped Abby to her feet.

"I'm gonna take you home girl."

"Oh Jake, I'm fearful sorry."

She wiped her eyes with her lace hankie.

"After you went to all the trouble of rentin' a horse and carriage, I've ruined it."

"No you haven't Abby. There'll be other times that the band will be playin'."

He helped her into the carriage, tucked the picnic basket under the seat and took her home.

Reaching the Oickle house, Jake snapped the reins over the back of the horse and maneuvered it around the circular driveway. Stepping down, he walked to Abby's side of the carriage to help her when the front door was thrown open and Mrs. Hull came running out. They stared dumbstruck at the sight of the plump cook running toward them screaming.

When she reached the carriage, she clung to Abby who had jumped down and ran toward her. Mrs. Hull bent over gasping for air trying to regain her breath while Abby stared at her completely bewildered.

"Oh Abby", she sobbed hysterically.

"What are we gonna do? What are we ever gonna do?"

"Abby come quickly. The walls, they're all bleedin'!"

Supporting her between them, they walked toward the open door. Abby tried to calm the sobbing woman.

"Don't be a feared Mrs. Hull, we're here."

As they entered the front foyer, the hair on Jake's arms stood ridged against his body and he felt his skin crawl over his bones. Abby, her eyes wide with horror, stood behind Jake squeezing his hands until they ached.

"Sweet mother of God! Listen."

It was as though a house full of grieving men, women and children were moaning and wailing for all the lost souls in the world. The heinous sound ran down Jake's spine paralyzing his body. Abby hung on to him, crossing herself and praying to all the saints for protection.

Mrs. Hull let out a piercing scream and pointed toward the wide staircase.

"Look at the walls. Oh my God, look at the walls!"

Horrified, they watched as saturated blotches appeared on the walls leading to the second floor. Blood covered the plaster before dripping to the wide oak stairs, pooling on the landing instead of disappearing like before. The carpeted steps became small waterfalls of crimson blood as the gory fluid splashed down on the marble foyer where they stood petrified.

The sound of demonic wailing and moaning throbbed from every fiber of the house. Jake fought against the mindless terror that was consuming him. Grabbing the terrorized women, he pushed them out the door and down the brick walk to safety.

They turned and watched through the open door as the evil fluid oozed towards them.

"There's no way you two are going to stay in this cursed house one more minute. I'm taking you to the Fairview Inn and you'll stay there 'til we get this figured out."

Abby stopped and pulled on his arms, her eyes glassy with hysteria.

"But Jake, we have to look after the house!"

He grabbed her shoulders and shook her hard.

"Are you out of your mind girl? You're not makin' any sense. Do you want to go back into that hellhole? Look at Mrs. Hull, she's had all she can handle and I'm not going to be answerable for what happens to you. I'm getting you both away from here now. This place is so evil, you can smell it."

Mrs. Hull screamed.

"Oh my God, it's coming after us!"

There in front of their eyes, a river of blood covered the brick entrance where they had stood just seconds before.

Jake half dragged, half carried them to the carriage. Groaning, he pushed and shoved Mrs. Hull up on the seat before helping a sobbing Abby. Jumping up, he squeezed in alongside of her. Grabbing the reins, he snapped them across the horses back. Shouting and driving the confused animal as fast as it would go, they rode to Bridgewater and the safety of the Fairview Inn.

Later, toward suppertime, Abby answered a knock on the door of their hotel room to find Jake and Ruben waiting outside.

"Hello Abby, I've brought Uncle with me. I think we got some talkin' to do."

Abby nodded, standing back for them to enter.

Almost in tears, Mrs. Hull sat rocking in a wicker chair that stood by the window overlooking Queen Street.

"Hello Ruben, I guess Jake told you what happened at the house this afternoon."

He sat down on the straight back chair across from her, shaking his head.

"He did Effie, but I still can't believe what he said."

"Oh believe it, because whatever he told you he saw at the door, was a whole lot worse from the inside. I've never seen or heard anything like it and I pray I don't have to go through it again."

Ruben leaned over and took Effie's hand.

"Well, I'll tell you one thing, you can't go back there tonight."

He groped in his pocket for his watch, pulling it out by the chain.

Why don't you and Abby come down to the dining room and have supper with Jake and me. Things will look different after a good meal. I don't think it's a good idea to go back to the house Effie. Not 'til we get this straightened up."

She stopped rocking and wiped a tear from the corner of her eye.

127

"It's almost suppertime."

"You're a good man Rueben. And I thank you for it."

Through the window, they could see forks of lightening illuminate the sky over the LaHave River.

He rose from the chair and stood in front of the window.

"Looks like there's a storm brewin'. I could feel it in the air when Jake and I walked over here."

He turned and watched as the cook wiped another tear from her cheek.

"We'll wait for you in the dining room and when you're ready you come down and join us."

By the time they had finished eating, the storm was gaining memento. Lightning ignited the murky sky as thunder rolled, charging the night air with deafening explosions. The roaring wind pounded so mercilessly against the side of the hotel that it sloshed the oil in the crystal lamps hanging on the walls.

Abby yawned daintily behind her hand before jumping almost out of her seat as more thunder exploded over their heads

"I'm tinkin' that my heart is going to jump right out, but I'm so tired that I don't care."

Jake squeezed her hand.

"No wonder, you've had a day to reckon with."

He watched as the lids on her green eyes began to droop.

Ruben nodded his head in agreement.

"The lad's right Effie. I think you and Abby should try to get a good night's sleep. It might be a problem with all the noise this storm is makin'."

The cook shook her head, yawning as well.

"The way I feel now, it would take more than this storm to keep me awake. Every bone in my body is craving rest."

Another deafening clap of thunder resounded, muffling the rain rattling on the sloping roof of the wide sweeping veranda.

Ruben grinned as he watched the rain pelting against the windows.

"You know Jake, there's a good chance that we might be wet by the time we get home tonight."

After they had escorted the women back to their room, they left the hotel. Ruben's prophecy had come true. By the time they scurried around the corner to Phoenix Street, they were both soaked to the skin from the pounding rain.

All through the night, the storm raged. In the morning, the residents of Bridgewater woke up to find that large trees had toppled to the ground causing destruction in their wake. A few barns in the settlement had gaping holes where their roofs use to be and small outbuildings that hadn't been sturdily built, lay battered on the ground; a lasting testimony of the storm's power.

Ruben sat behind his battered desk and watched as Jake applied the last coat of stain to a teak coffin.

"I hardly slept a wink last night Uncle, what with the storm howling outside. I just kept going over and over in my head what happened at the house. It just don't seem possible. But I'll tell you one thing right now, no girl of mine is goin' back to that hell house to work."

"I know lad, it's a strange business."

The banging of the workshop door interrupted their conversation. Jake threw his cloth down and went to unlock it. An excited Daniel Baker, followed him back inside.

"Morning Ruben. That storm pushed a tree branch blockin' your lane. I moved it for you before I came in."

Ruben nodded his head in thanks to the short plump man.

"I'm holdin' to you, Daniel. What brings you out so early after the storm?"

Daniel sat on a sawhorse and opened his coat. A man in his early forties, he owned the livery stable on Main Street, but his love of gossip out-weighed his love for horses. If Daniel Baker didn't know what was going on in the settlement of Bridgewater, then it wasn't worth knowing.

"I just heard some news. It's not good and it set me back some."

Jake, polishing the coffin, stopped and waited for him to continue.

"What's the news?"

"Well as far as we can gather, the storm last night sunk a ship headed toward Bridgewater from Liverpool. The latest word is that all hands were lost."

The coffin forgotten, Jake stood up balling the cloth in his hands.

"Who was it Dan? Did they say?"

He nodded his head.

"Yep, they did. They said that it was one of Edward Oickle's schooners."

Jake stood by the coffin, his cloth falling from his hand unnoticed.

"Dear God, man! You say everyone was lost?"

Daniel nodded his head sadly.

Jake swallowed hard and looked at his uncle.

"Did they say where it was comin' from?"

Daniel stood staring at the floor, with his hand running up and down his black suspenders.

"Come to think of it, they said that it was out of Boston."

He looked around for somewhere to get rid of his tobacco juice. Ruben noticing his discomfort, pointed to the brass spittoon standing in the corner. Daniel leaned over it and black juice arched through the air hitting its target right on.

"When did you find this out? "

"The news just came in a little while ago. Let me tell you, his office is in some upheaval, what with tryin' to find out more news before they announce it."

"You know whatever Edward touched made him money. People called him Lucky Eddy behind his back. Guess his luck ran out."

He leaned on the coffin that Jake had been polishing.

"Say, aren't you steppin' out with that pretty Irish girl that's workin' for him?"

Closing the lid, Jake nodded.

Daniel screwed up his face in concentration. His eyes almost disappearing in the rolls of fat that hung on his lids.

"Did she ever mention any strange goin's on at the house?"

Jake stood and looked Daniel straight in the eyes.

"No, she never mentioned one word to me. Why do you say that?"

The gossipmonger shook his head.

"Well if you never heard her say nothin', then it can't be true. I gotta go, but I thought you should know Ruben. You could be busy with the buryin', but I doubt it. The way those currents are off Crescent, them bodies will all be swept out to sea."

Daniel spit one more time and then left, leaving both men staring at each other.

"They're dead Uncle. I know that with every bone in my body. How are we gonna tell them?"

Ruben held his unlit pipe in his hand.

"I think that we should hold off 'til we know for sure. They've been through enough. You know you have to take everythin' that Daniel says with a grain of salt."

By noon, all of Bridgewater was buzzing with the news of the sinking of the "Della Mae". It was confirmed late afternoon that Edward Oickle, his wife and son had drowned, along with the crew, the night before off Crescent Beach.

Ruben and Jake set out for the Fairview Hotel with a heavy heart knowing that they would have to tell the news that everyone in the settlement now knew.

Jake could tell that Abby had been watching for them. The door swung back wide, even before they reached it. Her shy smile fading as she observed the somber expressions on their faces.

"Merciful saints! Somethin' terrible has happened. You better be tellin' us what it is."

They entered the room. Ruben rolled the brim of his straw hat around and around, trying to think of an easy way to break the news to them.

Effie sat on a wicker chair in the corner by the window, her hands covering her heart.

"Its bad news, isn't it Ruben?"

He picked up the straight back chair and placed it in front of the cook, nodding his head.

"I'm sorry Effie. A horrible thing happened last night or early this mornin' off the shores of Crescent Beach."

He paused and looked at Jake, who was leaning against the door watching Abby closely as she sat listening on the bed.

"Edward Oickle's schooner went down in the storm. I'm afraid, all hands were lost."

Abby gasped and whispered.

"Everyone?"

Ruben nodded.

"I'm afraid so girl. I'm sorry to say that it was the "Della Mae". Edward and his family were on that ship."

Effie started to cry softly.

"Oh those poor, poor people. They were such decent folk Ruben."

She slammed her hands on the arms of the rocking chair.

"I knew somethin' terrible was going to happen. That cursed house knew it too. Didn't it Abby?"

Abby walked wordlessly to the window, tears flowing unheeded as she gazed unseeingly at the street below.

Ruben stood up and placed his hand on Effie's shoulder.

"I'm sorry to break it to you like this, but there was no easy way. I want you to stay here 'til you get yourself situated. I'll look after the room. Jake and me will come back and have supper with you. They put on a good feed bag here."

He smiled down at her as she wiped more tears from her cheeks.

"Not as good as your table Effie, but passable all the same. By suppertime, more news will have come up the river, and you and the girl can decide what you're gonna do. We'll head back to the shop now."

She nodded her head. Her hands covering her face, muffled the wracking sobs. Helplessly his calloused hand patted her shoulder and then he left with Jake following behind him. He stood by the opened door crushing the brim of his hat with his fingers.

"Please don't worry. You and the girl will be okay."

Soft crying filtered out to the hall as they closed the door behind them.

They walked down the carpeted stairs to the lobby. Jake held the outer door open for his uncle and waited for him to pass before following him to the veranda.

"You know Uncle, I couldn't have done what you just did. That had to be a hard thing to do."

Ruben nodded, placing what use to be his second best hat on his head.

"We all have to do things in life that's hard lad. That's just how it is, but right now I'm thinkin' that this has be one of the saddest pieces of news I've ever had to break to anyone, let alone someone I think highly of."

Almost every household in the settlement was affected by the tragedy in Crescent Beach. By dusk an ominous apprehension had slithered into the homes, for another fall storm was raging outside.

In the dining room of the Fairview Hotel, they sat at a corner table and discussed the sad events of the day as another storm raged outside.

Abby crossed herself as a clap of thunder shook the dining room.

"Holy mother of God! That was a bad one."

Ruben shook his head, his face grim.

"You're right girl, it was." A crack like that means only one thing. "It hit somethin' big."

Abby crossed herself again.

"Just as long as it doesn't hit us. My da use to make us get up and hide under the table. It would get so bad in the old country. He use to say that the little people were having a fight and the terrible noise we heard was only the poundin' of the swords on the shields."

The thunder banged again, even louder than the last time. Disturbed faces watched through the large windows of the dining room as the heavens ignited around them.

Jake jumped and grinned with embarrassment.

"Whew! That one made my bones rattle."

After supper, the men kept them company in a smaller lounge of the hotel until most of the thunder had moved on. When they were satisfied that the women were out of danger, they said their goodbyes before heading into the torrential downpour.

Arriving home, Ruben entered the workshop and sat at his old battered desk, frowning at his unlit pipe. Puzzled, Jake watched as he tapped the blackened bowl in the palm of his hand.

"What's wrong Uncle? You look bothered. Are you worried about the storm? You said yourself that the worst has passed."

"It's not the storm that's bothering me, but what it will have left in its wake."

Next morning, Daniel Baker threw the door open rushing in.

"Ruben did you hear the news? Lightenin' hit two places last night and you're not gonna believe this, but one of those places was Edward Oickle's. Can you believe it man? It burned to the ground, every things gone. No one can call him Lucky Eddy now."

"Say that again!"

Jake's head shot up.

Daniel nodded his head.

"You heard it right the first time. The Oickle house burnt to the ground. Yep, his luck all ran out."

Running his hands up and down his wide black suspenders, he stood there shaking his head.

"But by God, did it have to all desert him at once?"

Daniel walked toward the door, pulling it open.

"I can't stay. I left the livery unattended, but I thought you should know."

When he left, the two men stood in silence. Ruben's hands shook slightly as he tried to light his pipe.

"Jake hitch up the wagon. We're goin' for a ride."

The journey out of Bridgewater was a challenge for both horse and driver. Heavy freight wagons squatted in the mud on Main Street, their huge wheels sunk to the hubs in the mucky mire.

Sliding back and forth on the road, Jake's lighter wagon steered around the heavier ones 'til he reached the outskirts of the settlement and a firmer road. Still, the going was challenging and his shoulders ached from handling the reins.

After what seemed like a long and tedious journey, Jake followed two of Edward's company wagons up the driveway to the smoldering ruins that had been Abby's home since she moved to Canada.

They sat on the top of the wagon and watched as Edward's hired men stumbled through the smoldering rubble. Kicking at the blackened skeletons of the elegant furniture, they roamed through the smoking ruins searching for hot spots to smother with the back of their shovels.

Ruben sat with his pipe lit in the nippy morning air and watched as a tall man with thinning red hair and bushy mutton sideburns waved and walked toward them. Stopped by different workmen, he answered numerous questions before reaching their wagon.

"Morning Ruben, Jake."

"Can you believe this? I'm findin' it hard to take in."

A look of intense sorrow crossed his face.

Ruben shook his head sadly as he and Jake climbed down from the high seat of the wagon. Placing his hand on the grieving man's shoulder, he gave it a squeeze.

"These are trying times for you Archie, that's for sure. You were like brothers."

Archie's eyes darkened with unshed tears. He turned his head and stared at the river below.

"That we were Ruben that we were."

They stood silently watching the men push down the last wall. Sparks flew around the workers as the front of the house crashed into the smoldering remains of the once beautiful home.

"Were you able to save anything?"

"The only thing that we found was little Neddy's rockin' horse. I...I gave him that horse for his third birthday."

He gazed toward the river again.

"Now the only thing left is the view."

Ruben lifted his arm and waved it around.

"He sure had a nice spread here."

Archie nodded, still watching the river. Abruptly, he turned staring straight into the face of the older man. He weighed his words carefully.

"Yup he did... but you know, things aren't always what they seem."

Jake and Archie's eyes locked. Jake held his breath and waited for his uncle's next words.

"What makes you say that?"

"Edward and me have been friends for a long time. He made me manager of his whole operation because of the trust we had between us. It was part of my job to oversee the buildin' of the house before they moved in, 'cause he was away so much on buyin' trips. I was proud that he asked me to look after it. Well... when we got diggin' the foundation, we found that somebody had dug there before us... 'cause we found bones."

He looked around, lowering his voice so that only the two men leaning against the muddy wagon could hear.

"Human bones, Ruben. It was enough of them that it looked like some kind of graveyard. I told Eddy that we should stop diggin' here, but he wouldn't listen to me. He told me to get rid of them and to keep on with the house."

Ruben glanced at Jake, nodding his head.

"Ah... that would explain... a lot."

Archie knocked his muddy boots on the wagon wheel.

"I didn't want to Ruben, but I did it anyway. Eddy said that this was the prettiest part of the river and bones or no bones he was buildin' here. Later I found some buttons and other scrapes that looked like it could to be French. You know that they came up this river some hundred years ago, called it the LaHave and then left. I guess some didn't get to leave with the rest."

Shaking his head, Ruben grabbed the side of the seat and pulled himself up on the wagon.

"That wasn't smart thinkin' on Edward's part."

"I know it wasn't."

Jake pointed to the men working in the ruins.

"How did you keep them from talkin' 'bout what they found?"

"That was the easy part. All the regular men were busy unloading Eddie's ships, so I hired a crew just to dig out the foundation. They came in on one of the schooners that landed here to take on provisions, and the men were willing to make some extra money. So word just never got around. The bonus I gave them didn't hurt either."

Archie pulled a plug of chewing tobacco out of his pocket, along with a knife offering to share it with them. Both men declined. Placing it in the corner of his mouth, he continued.

"You know, along with them Frenchy bones we found some things that told us that Indians were buried here too."

Ruben drew on his pipe, his eyes meeting Jakes.

"So he built himself a fine house on top of a graveyard, did he? I always thought Edward was a lot smarter than that, but from what I heard, he sure proved me wrong."

Archie watched Ruben keenly. Astonishment flooded his face. He realized that they knew the horrible truth about the walls, the truth that Edward had tried so hard to keep from the settlement.

Ruben puffed on his pipe while Jake moved the reins from one hand to the other.

"What's going to happen to the property?"

Archie shrugged his shoulders.

"Right now I don't know for sure. Maybe it will have to go up for sale."

Ruben puffed on his pipe again. The curling gray smoke hung motionless in the crisp air.

"What did you do with the bones that you found?"

"Well... I gathered them all up and I placed them in the north corner of the foundation. I figured they'd be out of the way."

"You know what I'd do if I were you, Archie?"

He pointed with his pipe to the land around him.

"I'd dig those bones back up and when you got them all, you come to me and I'll make sure that I have a couple of coffins ready for you."

He puffed one last time on his pipe and then knocked it against the side of the wagon.

"Then we'll do what should have been done in the beginnin'. We'll bury them in a proper grave. It will be a secret that the three of us will share."

He scrutinized the cleared land around them.

"I think that it would be a real shame for the next owner to have the same heartbreak that Edward's family had to handle. What do you say, Archie?"

He looked up at the undertaker and seconds seem to pass into minutes before he nodded.

"I'll get right at it, Ruben."

"I know you will. It's just too bad that it wasn't done before. This could be a different story here now."

He shook his head, his expression grim, as he slapped both of his thighs with the flat of his hands.

"Let's head for home, Lad."

Jake snapped the reins on the horse's rump and they headed back to Phoenix Street, a lot wiser than when they had left.

They sat on the veranda of the hotel enjoying one of the last balmy afternoons of autumn. Gangly flowers that stood in colorful clumps against the side of the hotel only yesterday, lay sprawled on the ground. Their blackened leaves, a testimony to the heavy frost from the night before.

Jake listened as his uncle told the women about the fire and the foreman's tale of the bones. He was astonished at how well they took the news for they had lost everything they possessed in the fire.

"I'm sorry Effie, but everythin' went up in smoke. The lad here thought that there might be somethin' left that we could save for you, but it's all gone."

Effie sighed as a tear rolled down her cheek.

"They were just things, Ruben. When our time on earth is done, we can't take them with us."

Abby nodded her head. Ruben sat back on a Boston rocking chair puffing on his pipe, his hand patting Effie's.

"I know Effie, but you and the girl lost everythin' when the house went up in smoke."

Watching Abby and Jake sitting quietly on the wicker love seat holding hands, she smiled sadly.

"It's probably best that it burned. The place was cursed. They were just things, Ruben. A person can get tired of draggin' them around."

Ruben watched as Jake and Abby walked hand in hand down the front steps of the hotel. Grinning, he watched them jump around the water puddles on Queen Street. Ruben puffed on his pipe and then removed it from his mouth tapping the warm bowl in the palm of his hand, while Effie rocked beside him. He cleared his throat.

"You know Effie, we've known each other for a longtime and I've been told that I'm a might set in my ways."

Lifting his hand, he pointed in the direction of the younger couple.

"The lad there will tell you that in a heartbeat."

He grinned at the startled look on her face.

"But we've spent a lot of time in each other's space lately and I can tell you that even with this horrible thing hangin' over your head, you've been fine company. And I... well I was wonderin'... if you might want to spend the rest of your life with me. What do you say Effie?"

She stopped rocking and sat very still. Her head bent, she caressed the gold band on her third finger. After a moment of silence, she hesitated and then took Ruben's calloused hand and smiled at a very nervous undertaker.

"You're right, we have known each other a long time. You're a fine and honorable man, Ruben and I would be proud to carry your last name."

He grinned and squeezed her hand.

"I thank you, Effie. I got a feelin' in my bones that we won't be the only two newlyweds living on Phoenix Street."

She laughed, watching Jake carry a giggling Abby over a mud puddle.

"You know Ruben, I think you're right."

The clunking sound of a pick hitting the hard packed earth, echoed in the still dusk air above the river. Archie leaned over the gaping hole.

"Want me to take over?"

Jake threw the shovel and pick up into the air and watched as they landed on the mound of damp earth.

"No, I'm done. Give me a hoist Archie, I've been in this hole long enough."

He wrapped both hands around Jake's and pulled him from the grave.

Hearing a noise, they stared at each other with dread.

"Lordy Jake, you hear that?"

Jake nodded his head, almost afraid to speak.

"I hear it. It's a wagon headed this way."

Jake glared at his friend.

"I know what it is Archie. How are we gonna explain these here holes?"

They stood helplessly by the graves. The rattling of the wheels came closer to the crest of the hill. As it reached the top of the drive, they recognized Ruben and they sagged with relief. The wagon came to an abrupt stop in front of the graves. Reverend Duff and Ruben jumped down and stood by the two holes. Ruben pointed to the back of the wagon.

"The coffins are under the canvases in the back. I hope they're big enough."

Archie and Jake pulled the coffins from the wagon and placed them next to the empty graves. Ruben pulled off the lids and waited until the younger men dragged two large, heavy bags from the back of Archie's wagon. Half lugging, half carrying the burlap shrouds, they laid the bones of the early explorers beside the waiting coffins.

Archie apologized to Reverend Duff.

"The bones were all jumbled together Reverend when we dug them up, so me and Jake put them in new bags."

Reverend Duff smiled reassuringly.

"You did fine Archie."

They placed the bagged bones into the coffins. Ruben pulled a small hammer and several nails from his coat pocket and nailed the lids securely to the sides.

Dusk was settling as Reverend Duff removed his prayer book from his satchel. He waited until the disturbed bones were lying at the bottom of their new graves before offering a prayer and blessing for both the resting place and its contents.

The hollow sound of heavy, wet earth hitting wood reverberated in the still of the twilight.

Ruben and the reverend stood together watching as Jake and Archie threw the last shovel of dirt on the graves, forever covering the bones.

Collecting their tools, they embarked on the short ride back to the settlement.

Dusk stepped aside for a cool, starlit night. The wagons followed close behind each other, as the horses cautiously eased their way along the dark, rutted road.

Exhausted, Jake slumped against the seat.

"Do you think it made a difference Uncle? Did we put them to rest?"

Ruben pulled back on the reins, the wagon rattling to a stop. Clenching the unlit pipe between his teeth, he stared at the blackened skeletal remains of a house that was once filled with love and life.

In the haunting shadows of a rising moon, wispy, gray mist swirled and danced above the foreboding graves.

"One can only hope Jake... one can only hope."

THUNDER RUMBLED IN the distance, while the spent wind nudged the last of the storm clouds away. For long moments, the stranger stared out the window. Stillness settled over the inhabitants of the inn as they waited for another story.

A spark shot from the hearth landing by his feet. Startled, a woman screamed. Lifting his hobnailed boot over it, he ground the dying ember into the floor. Once more, he stared out the window as if searching for something. Taking a swig of ale, he turned another page and read on.

About Heather D. Veinotte

Playwright Heather D. Veinotte has written and directed more than 26 plays for radio and stage. As well as being a recognized playwright, she is the author of two novels, "The Mystery on Skull Island"-A young reader book and "Beyond the Mist", a paranormal set in the 1800's in and near the historic towns of Lunenburg and Mahone Bay. Heather's very proud of the fact that this novel was awarded Honorable Mention in the prestige Writers' Digest Competition of North America. She was born in Bridgewater, Nova Scotia, the eldest of three children. Her love of stories began at a very early age when she would sit by her grandfather on his porch swing and listened enthralled as he wove tales about the "olden days" in Lunenburg County. Heather discovered the joy of books at a very early age. Along with the reading came the overwhelming passion to write, which she has never lost. She married her soul mate Bruce and together they have a son, daughter and two grandsons. They live in West Northfield, a charming community on the South Shore of Nova Scotia.